THE PAINTED ROOM

ALSO BY INGER CHRISTENSEN

alphabet
Azorno
Butterfly Valley
The Condition of Secrecy
it
Light, Grass, and Letter in April
Natalja's Stories

INGER CHRISTENSEN

THE PAINTED ROOM

a tale of Mantua

TRANSLATED FROM THE DANISH
BY DENISE NEWMAN

A New Directions Paperbook Original

Copyright © 1976 by Inger Christensen & Brøndums Forlag
Copyright © 2000, 2025 by Denise Newman

Published by arrangement with Gyldendal Group Agency

All rights reserved.
Except for brief passages quoted in a newspaper, magazine,
radio, television, or website review, no part of this book
may be reproduced in any form or by any means,
electronic or mechanical, including photocopying and recording,
or by any information storage and retrieval system, or be used
to train generative artificial intelligence (AI) technologies
or develop machine-learning language models,
without permission in writing from the Publisher.

First published as New Directions Paperbook 1633 in 2025
Manufactured in the United States of America

Library of Congress Control Number: 2025006303

2 4 6 8 10 9 7 5 3 1

New Directions Books are published for James Laughlin
by New Directions Publishing Corporation
80 Eighth Avenue, New York 10011

Contents

I

THE DIARIES
OF MARSILIO ANDREASI

a selection

1454

Now, in this hour, begins the systematic destruction of my beloved Nicolosia.

Now she is placed on the pine bench of wedlock and is stretched and bent until she has pushed out an adequate number of sons. I cannot understand it.

I cannot understand how those kinds of arrangements are thought to be necessary in a time when it is so openly the fashion to get quantities of illegitimate children, not only to brag about their mere existence, but also and essentially to wager on those products that achieve a reasonable quality. Which is honest enough. At certain junctures, it is even an idealistic and sensible thing.

Therefore I cannot understand the morbid logic that in these circumstances demands the sequestration of a woman as one of its sick consequences, nor the need to isolate her in a kind of philosophical forcing house where birth, death, and violence are blended according to the simplest domestic recipe ever handed down. The resultant dish is called life-enhancing, mystical, healthy. Poor Nicolosia! If we venture into this field at all we become fathers in any event.

In my despair I have even invoked the Heavenly Father, the World's Actuary, hoping that in His wisdom He would enter up the reckoning for my beloved in such a way that she would be unable to produce issue — sons or otherwise — in her forced marriage.

But deep in my heart I am in doubt: Why should He (as the only one) stretch out his hand to me, a simple secretary, in his lofty insouciance? He is not to know that this secretary is a writer in his free time and, as such, an actual protégé of heaven.

He is not to know because I never reveal myself.

He cannot even know I have my reasons for it, that I cast a jaundiced eye upon the present conditions, with every other secretary at least and soon every fifth doctor and lawyer, not to mention any number of carpenters and other down-to-earth people, cavorting about our squares and piazzas and fanning each other on the nose with their latest poems.

My attitude about this whole wretched business has long been that it is too late to speak up when God and everyone else just talks and talks and nobody listens anymore.

If only we had married the first time we saw each other.

Spring is awful. The Mincio flows in over the island as if over a plate, leaving behind its rats, its mud, and its gasping fish. This is the type of reward nature gives its loyal cultivators.

Baldassare came in from the villa crying yesterday. The rain had torn the blossoms off the treetops and there will be a dearth of almonds and olives. What should a gardener do on the waves of sin? he screamed.

Yes, what should a fisherman do in the desert? Or a stonemason in heaven? Or the angel in the fire of earthly feelings? What should he do?

19th April. Evening

It is best to no longer call yourself a human being. But in the silence of your heart to talk to yourself as if to a sphinx, a machine, or a monk.

20th April

Sat in the Hall of the Sun today listening to Bartholomeo.

Both Gianfrancesco and Rodolfo were present. As always when there are catastrophes in the air they were in a cheerful mood. If only it were they and not their father who had charge of the castle's affairs, many things would look differently. First and foremost, my accounts.

We were drinking wine from the Kuri's fields on the Capitol, vintage 1444. It had gone off.

"Dear Bartholomeo Manfredi, tell us about mankind," sneered Rodolfo.

"Yes, tell us about crop failure and the lists of sins," said Gianfrancesco as he poured the wine. "About ruins and disappointed hopes."

He is like his mother. A true Hohenzollern. Practical and morose.

I sat thinking about the ruins on the Capitol. About how only fifteen years ago the entire complex had been overgrown with hawthorn and acanthus and how the Pope had sent his vintner monks up there with instructions not to return before they were able to bring him back a jar of the Capitol's wine.

"When something is necessary why do we not do it?" said Rodolfo.

They were now speaking about the floods which would occur in 1455 and 1456 and 1457, continuing in this way every spring into eternity.

"It is because chance enters into it," said Bartholomeo.

"That is no excuse," they said with one voice and laughed, as if that put them in agreement about everything.

"No, it is no excuse," said Bartholomeo. "Not at all. Everything is preconditioned by the game of chance. But people forget that rationality is only one system among many others. They forget that the world is moving on. They believe it stands still while they sit down and ponder."

"What does Bartholomeo Manfredi mean by the world?" said Rodolfo obsequiously.

"As a mathematician I am concerned only with mapping out the logical entities and the way they move," he said coldly, "so they will no longer get in the way of intuition."

"Intuition! I'll drink to that!" said Gianfrancesco.

Vintage 1444 is one of the very first from the Capitol. To begin with, the wine gives one a lift, but afterwards its vengeance is dire.

After this we began to talk about the past, about all the visionary projects that never came to anything because while the war would have justified their being carried into effect, it never broke out at precisely the right place and time to require the project to be realized.

And Rodolfo told the same old story about the tyrant from Milan and his partiality for the colossal.

How, for the price of 300,000 gold guilders, he carried out the most fantastic dam projects that would have enabled him to divert the Mincio from Mantua and the Brenta from Padua at will and, in a matter of a few hours, put these cities at his mercy. But all his great engineering works remained unfinished.

"If only they existed," said Gianfrancesco, "then Mantua would be spared this eternal flooding."

"Then Mantua would not exist. Then the tyrant would have long ago annihilated the future which we are now living in," said Bartholomeo. "As soon as a so-called tyrant comes into possession of an instrument of destruction you can be sure it will be used."

"Desperate ills need desperate remedies," said Rodolfo, foolish as he is.

And that is where it was left. The floods should be banished by drought and the drought by flooding, war by peace, and peace again by disputes and riots and popular insurrections.

21st April

When I look at what I have written from our conversation yesterday, I really feel that we are grappling with matters far above our station.

Also the wine, which we drank again today, makes me feel ashamed. I was actually present at the time when Lodovico was delivered the jars by the papal carriage and in his bombastic excitement vowed that they should be reserved for his wake.

True, he could not know and does not know the wine is sour.

But neither could Gianfrancesco and Rodolfo know if one day a miracle, maybe at the moment of death, were to turn the wine from the Capitol into pure nectar.

Tomorrow I will check on the jars and balance the accounts.

12th May

Federico has come home from Venice bringing the first report of Nicolosia Bellini's marriage to Andrea Mantegna.

(undated)

Oh my God and Creator, make me deformed so that my heart and mind will be visible to your eye.

Today I could no longer keep silent.

During the last year Lodovico has requested me to draw up no fewer than ten so-called letters or petitions to this Mantegna.

I cannot describe what sorrow this has woken in my mind, having to attend to these shrieking letters.

To see such a magnanimous and lovable person as the Prince of Gonzaga humiliating himself to such a degree for a simple and stubborn painter has been one of the greatest trials during my employment here in Mantua.

Why do we not appoint Storlato to the position of court painter? He is a sociable man and has painted both God the Father and the Twelve Apostles many times.

Or Il Pannonio? Why do we not send for him? He has the necessary delicacy. But of course no one would expect that from someone who has grown up in Hungary.

Might it be better to have grown up in Squarcione's

workshop, where the only muses are impudence, deceit, and profit?

Many times I have heard Squarcione give the young apprentices orders to sneak into other workshops around the city and steal their good ideas or copy their latest creations.

This is how both Pizzolo and Mantegna were taught arrogance, brutality, and the hunt for novelty.

This I also said to Gonzaga. Why appoint a troublemaker? I said. Just look what happened to Pizzolo. He was murdered. So why appoint the murderer's closest friend so long as the murderer remains at large?

But Gonzaga has taken no account of my suggestions. He simply persists with his idolatry and furthermore has applied to the Protonotary Apostolic Gregorio Correr, as well as to prominent public officials in Padua, in letters that almost amount to bribery, asking them to use their influence on the divine decorator. As if these high-ranking officials were temple servants in some interior-design workshop.

Within the past few months the Gonzaga family's offer to Mantegna has increased fivefold. Amounts that have little to do with reality.

The good Fancelli will have something to say about this. He has not received his salary since the spring, despite the fact that in August he was ordered to travel to Padua at the height of the plague, with all manner of threats if he did not save the great artist from dying like a fly and remove him to safety behind the walls of Mantua as soon as possible.

Why risk Luca Fancelli's life in order to save Mantegna's? Is an architect suddenly worth less than a painter? After all, the walls have to be designed and erected before they can be painted on.

Moreover, what did Fancelli find when he reached the painter's house? He found a man who had pawned his wife's ring in order to be able to survive and remain self-sufficient. He found a man who refused to open his door to a worthy delegate from Mantua's court; a man who had sealed up his house with plaster and terra-cotta and who shouted so loudly through the sealed door Fancelli got plaster in his eyes. "I am not dealing with infected architects," he shouted. "Let the whole benighted city fall to ruin. I take my stand on the light in my pictures." Poor Nicolosia!

Yes, it really looks as if Lodovico will go down in history as a mild and thoughtful prince with a propensity for bizarre ideas and artistic abominations.

As for me, for the time being I am excused from composing letters and nothing apart from the daily accounts prevents me from completing my treatise "On the Relationship Between Intuition and the Art of Calculation."

In connection with this, I finally started counting the jars of the Capitol wine. There were 250 half-gallon jars. Thus, exactly half of the original gift of one thousand quarts of wine. So Lodovico should not have too many illusions about an unforgettable wake.

1460

Mantegna arrived at a quarter to two, visibly plagued by the heat and by his three dogs, each of them practically man-high; they were half-wild with thirst and licking the salty sweat off his hands and throat.

He was alone. He had left his family and the rest of the company behind with a wine grower northeast of Villafranca so they could rest for a day and organize their people and their possessions: the evening before, they had been out in a violent cloudburst in the already waterlogged terrain west of Zevio.

I hate him.

As a rule these artists reveal themselves to be conservative upstarts in their actual behavior. They take pride in defying the elements to no useful purpose.

Mantegna was no exception as he stood there in the courtyard almost completely encrusted in mud and unable to say a word because of the filth and exhaustion.

If you had not seen him move you might have thought that the entire Mantuan court had been ordered to salute one of the effigies brought to light in the excavations at Clusium, in some novel act of devotion.

Everyone was called out and the place was swarming with children and women and livestock. It is amazing how many creatures we are hiding in our houses.

But it was not until Bartholomeo Manfredi was summoned from his tower and introduced as the learned mechanic that I became truly disgusted: Lodovico really has no sense of proportion.

It is all too much when we have a God-given mathematician and he is put in the shade simply because a picture maker happens along who has shown a little sensitivity and taste.

If the State, with its thinkers and seers, were to be cast down in the dust on account of its sensuality and its selfish dreams, then I should rather see Baldassare the gardener lead Mantua back to its condition of original innocence.

Fancelli was beside himself; he gave a sickening display of superstition in its latest form — he brought in two bowls with honey and garlic, and when Mantegna was suddenly racked with a shiver which could probably be interpreted as nausea, Fancelli threw himself to the ground and kissed the man's boots, for no apparent reason. But among those who knew what was what, here was a sign that from now on he would place this ague-ridden painter on the same level as his lord and master, Leon Battista Alberti, who for many years has been authorized to call himself a genius.

A genius so all-embracing that along with everything in the world that he has mastered there are only two small, innocent things that he has not: honey and garlic. At the sight of them Mantegna promptly throws up, gets a fever, and has to sleep for days. Like a jilted mistress.

To do him justice I have to say that Mantegna took scarcely any notice of this display of emotion; at dinner he ate both a beefsteak studded with garlic and focaccia with honey.

17th August

Today I finally caught a glimpse of Nicolosia. I became deathly pale and could barely move. My brain turned completely white and my heart was so drained of blood that it could hardly beat; and I froze. An angel in the fire of earthly feelings.

1464

Mantegna returned this evening from his trip to Lake Garda and my time in heaven is over.

In less than five months we have lived a whole life. She like a flower among flowers. I like a bee among bees. In the garden of paradise.

All happiness is now collected and deposited in death as the fire is in the sun.

24th September

Nothing can affect the melting sphinx.

5th October

For days and nights there have been parties and discussions, sad and witty, conceited and beautiful, in a sort of blending that has never before been the fashion.

Feliciano is really a delightful person.

Evening after evening he has been chuckling as he listens to Antenorea's sober accounts of the expedition, and with his laughter he sheds light on its obscurer passages, while all along, without it in any way becoming apparent to us, he has been composing the most wonderful songs in his ingenious head, songs about nature and the rebirth of humanity.

Tonight, after Antenorea had told about their last solemn outing on Lake Garda under sail, he sang about the snow on the highest mountain that melts so slowly, as if constantly holding back its tears, as if it was in league with the sun and was more fire than water.

"This is the way we should live," said Mantegna, who, apart from this, did not contribute much to the conversation. He still wore the wreath of flowers with which Feliciano had adorned him a few months ago, that day in May when they arrived at the southern shore of the lake and had immediately taken the newest branches from the trees to build a temple where they pretended to be shepherd animals — as Feliciano described them — and set to worshipping the holy Virgin and her Son, the shining Thunder God, while rain poured down from a cloudless sky.

That wreath, however, is the only visible result that the expedition returned with. Unless you include the aura of devotion which has reigned over Mantegna since their return, as though he is watching a secret of which he knows nothing and which will escape his mortal frame forever if he is subjected to the slightest agitation.

The other unknown painter, Samuele da Tradate, who was also on the trip, has made much of the fact that the expedition accomplished nothing.

Already from the first evening he insisted that we call him Sam, short for Sesame, because he regarded his own self as being the magic word that could penetrate nonexistence.

And he had spent a whole night drawing the labyrinth they had dreamed of finding in the cemetery at Clusium but never found, probably because it has existed exclusively in Pliny's imagination as a dream of making a depiction of history.

We could not find the labyrinth, said Sam with a meaningful look, simply because it can never be found, because it is neither in Clusium nor anywhere else, it is everywhere: we are forever within the labyrinth and, as a matter of fact, ought to have a more compelling reason to believe that we are able to find it than we realize. But it never comes to pass, since, at every step we take, the labyrinth moves with us in the same direction at exactly the same pace.

Lodovico Gonzaga blazed up like a dragon after this outpouring and swept up the whole party in a round dance through the castle. Finally the women surrendered to their natural element and let themselves be carried like birds through endless galleries.

Lodovico flew in front; he was at once ecstatic and controlled, a relatively rare combination, but it is always present in the father figure. He is ready to release all his strength and magnificence in the very moment when his sons set their finger on the riddle of existence that, for life's sake, has to be made comprehensible no matter how unattainable, no matter how simple it is.

Lodovico is right. The best way to proceed is to let the dragon go into the labyrinth and out again; once happily out again, it makes a circuit round the empty, solitary interior. Slowly the secret reverts to secrecy while the experience is forgotten.

N. has not been present these evenings. He keeps her shut up in Via Mazzoni where Lodovico has provided him with a house for the time being. Under no circumstances will he take up residence in the castle. He demands a piece of land that he can call his own, and where he — this is my insertion — can guard his eccentricities as if they were the Kingdom of Heaven.

Tonight I was thinking how these intentions are written all over his face. He looks like something between a bright errand boy and a cherub, and you cannot help respecting him, but all the better to ensnare him when the time comes.

I find it highly unlikely that he should ever fall into his own trap. An archangel whose hand is shaking so much that the flaming sword sets fire to his hair or coat is unfortunately not to be imagined.

6th October

Yesterday I forgot to note the little sequel to the dance.

Tradate was asked what he meant when he said that his own self was the word that could penetrate nonexistence.

He was visibly confused by the question and could do no more than repeat what he had already said.

Painters are strange; they talk nearly all the time, but when they are asked to express themselves about something specific, they fall silent, as though under a sudden snowfall of images and visions.

I happened to be reminded of the famous words uttered by the blessed Pius II as he was whirling into Mantua for the Congress of '59, borne on his way by the twelve bastards from Este who were riding hell for leather so that the snow-white beasts were frothing at the mouth; with a squeaky voice, which carried right over the sound of the hoofbeats and the human din, the Pope could be heard exclaiming: "Within the storm the storm is a cloud that stands still."

In the same way Tradate succeeded in giving expression to what he meant; for while Antenorea and

Manfredi staggered under the burdensome problem of nonexistence, he drew the room we sat in, drew the opening out into the misty morning landscape, drew the people present, but did not draw us in the room at the tables where we sat. He drew us as pictures on the walls, from where we looked at the room with the empty chairs and the tables which were also empty, with the exception of one, namely the one at which Tradate was actually sitting; on it he drew an apple and a knife so lifelike that all the pictured people's mouths watered at the sight of it.

Nobody else saw the drawing because they were all caught up in the entertainment provided by Antenorea and Manfredi's wild reasoning, which went more or less like this:

"There is no difference between existence and nonexistence. Nonexistence is only a word, but the word is always a person, and the person is the dimension in the human being that lives in love for what is not yet created, for what is lacking. What is lacking is the Soul, or God, and before we have created them, we are forced to believe that there is a difference between existence and nonexistence."

1468

It is hard to believe that Bernardino is already three
years old. He is the most beautiful child you can imagine, and in the workshop he, of course, is allowed
to do everything. He is even allowed to take those
large slabs of marble with Roman inscriptions, which
Mantegna has otherwise guarded so zealously, and
use them for a pallet.

The peacocks have arrived.

The dream that grows in the sleeper's life.

The dream about a future.

But there is no future. There is only human kind,
this overwhelming society which looks like a spirit in
revolt. An abyss whose walls are lined with every con-
ceivable (and inconceivable) value, like Shrovetide
mechanisms falling to decay.

On appropriate occasions such values are taken

up and put in order, and one afternoon, usually in the spring, when the Church or some other ruling land-owner has the time, they are made to take wing — to no effect: they are weighed down by people who possess nothing, by people bereft of all joy save for such ones as may befuddle their brains to numb their sorrows.

The Prince not only tolerates such behavior but actually encourages it, as he deftly conceals his true purposes: that everyone should be allowed to feel as if they had wings; all flying machines, in the likeness of Mary's Assumption and other incomprehensible flights through space, are generally conceived of as images of good Fortune; thus everyone, by finally regarding themselves as possessing something of value, will feel happy without being so. Everyone except the Prince. His privilege is always to feel unfortunate without ever being so.

With an evenhandedness that is labeled strategy by some modern theorists, every move towards revolution is entered into the balance sheet of Power. Any sign of enthusiasm that might arise in Venice, Milan, or Padua, and in the surrounding lands that depend on these cities, is entered into the ledger against the total sum of effort, of consolation, of artistic fulfillment.

Seen from this perspective it matters little whether there is war or peace. Around this time twenty-five years ago we celebrated the conclusion of peace in Lodi and never understood that we celebrated in vain.

In time of war, people are more inclined to stick together and, having secured their ground, they have no need to fight day in day out to maintain it; they can live a life of strength and peace and spare a thought for others.

In time of peace, on the other hand, when all these arrogant fighting men return with their envy and their inaptitude for civil government, one is forever being challenged with dire calls to arms and time-wasting initiatives.

Thus, for every step we take, the abyss moves with us, and I needs must implore my Lord and Maker, the Mercy Killer, to fling me down into this chalice and this time let me follow my perdition right to the bottom.

(The Land of the Dead is the Prince's utopia.)

27th July

Today, at last, we received a letter from Mantegna's house. Just as I said: That man is crazy. Practically all last year he frittered away his time overseeing the preparations for the large cemeteries in Pisa, and the year before that he was loafing around in Florence giving instructions for decorating cellars and crypts that were wringing wet; and now, when at last he is right here in Mantua where he is paid to be, he sends Gonzaga a letter implying that he has locked himself in his house to paint "a story all about Limbo."

We pay him to deliver miracles of beauty, to identify the similarities between the best of our dreams and the physical world, not to get himself bogged down in reflections on death, nightmares, and burial ceremonies however ingenious. The place for Death is in one's private diary, it has no place in Art.

1st August

The auditorium is still empty. The three weavers have begun to play cards, and the tapestries will not be finished before Mantegna has drawn the peacocks bought for that purpose and which cry at night so that no one can sleep; they cry so piercingly that the women of the households are beginning to take auguries from them and to use those lecherous-eyed feathers to fan the faces of the sick. I do not know whether their hope is to fan the soul in or out.

They have even treated the Duchess Barbara with these ridiculous feather twitches even though all she was sick from was sorrow and resentment. She, who has a broader concept of the State than all men and philosophers, has now lost two of her sons to the

Church. When the youngest, Lodovico, was enthroned as Bishop in Mantua on his ninth birthday, the Duchess, blinded by tears, threw herself into the river.

She was rescued by the senior class in Vittorini's nature school — they were studying carp and the transmigration of souls. They say these fish become so incredibly old because they are able to gather soul material in their flesh.

Ever since, Barbara gets the girls to make a wreath out of pancratium and oak leaves every day, which she throws into the river while mumbling curses on the Church that locks children up inside themselves.

The other day I saw Mantegna sneak after her and make a sketch of the unfortunate woman. He has had a commission since '64 to make a portrait of the Duchess and now he chooses to begin one in this situation when she is beside herself with despair. Such capriciousness can only be a sign of mental illness.

But Gonzaga is not open to talking about these things. Let me give just one example: Mantegna has on several occasions signed his name "Comes Palatinus," and everyone expected he would be dismissed, reprimanded, or punished in some way, but what did Gonzaga do? He made Mantegna a Count on the spot and granted him new parcels of land and sufficient funds to begin the construction of a house of his own.

He has been here eight years and has not so much as drawn a peacock. It is an inexplicable scandal. As late as today a letter was sent off to Count Alliprandi saying that Gonzaga set greater store by Mantegna's big toe than by any of the people who had complained. And this despite the fact that Alliprandi had submitted his complaint on behalf of all the neighbors. Poor Nicolosia! Poor Bernardino!

1472

The Cardinal will spend the summer near the Baths at Poretta. He must take the waters to help his respiration and his feverish humors that, during the winter especially, give him skin eruptions and itchiness in one place and another. He has requested a visit from Mantegna, probably to obtain an estimate of the value of his precious collection of jewels and antiques which always accompany him on his travels.

In a way he is the one son who clings most passionately to the things of this world. I believe it might be this anxiety at having to let go that sets up those irritations to his skin. There is an old proverb that, in my childhood, only the women used, and even then only when the men were out of earshot. They would say it, for example, when we were being bathed in the evening, or when we were being dressed for the Easter party. They would look us in the eyes and say: "The human body is the most beautiful image of the Soul. Yes, it is the Soul itself."

I cannot imagine us men ever finding the courage

to use this proverb. Maybe in discussing philosophy, but never in the course of everyday life.

21st July

Mantegna has left, and work on the new audience chamber has been suspended. This afternoon when I went to lock it up I found Nana in there with seven of the peacocks. It sounded as if she were speaking their language, and they had placed themselves in a circle around her and sat listening to the peacocks' god.

29th July

I am visiting Nicolosia again. But it is no longer as it was that time in the garden of paradise. No more of that longing, not for what lies behind us, or ahead; not even the thought of the life we might have lived saddens us any more. On the contrary, we feel very lonely together.

In the presence of people of rank I have been called a fanatic, and because I am still unmarried and it is my temperament to treat other people as brothers, the mob has lost all inhibition and has often called me "boy lover."

Even though I have never, except in my early optimistic childhood, touched a soul other than Nicolosia.

Maybe Nicolosia is disgusted to think that I have never married.

In the same way, in spite of my lifelong attempt to become one with my angel, I am still disgusted by the fact that Nicolosia is married. We never speak of the children.

Have started to argue with Nicolosia. Also about Mantegna. Or Andrea, as she stubbornly calls him, as if he were a child.

Today it was his drawings for the new house that made us lose our tempers. She believes she will like living in the new house. I know she will be unhappy there as she is here, but there even more so.

To judge from the drawings, it is a prison, an isolated cubicle some eighty feet square, without any openings to the outside world other than a camouflaged entrance: it will be painted to look as if it is made of rock, and the door handle will be part of a pattern in relief.

The vestibule, the rotunda, and the large room in the middle of the garden facade are reserved for the artist and his work, it is less a living space than a workshop, and not even an ordinary workshop, rather a sort of shrine to beauty or, as Mantegna calls it in his notes, "a meeting place for admirers." Whether it is he himself who is to be admired or beauty in general is unfortunately not made clear.

If I know him aright, he has delusions of grandeur as do so many of the vagrant brats the state has adopted. Not by installing them in society. The upper class is too timid and too canny to do that. No, by letting them install themselves as a separate, self-governing association, like the Church; so these are two areas in which talent and a fervent fear of God are all that counts. And following quite another sequence of numbers than generally obtains. Perhaps following the metadimensions of mathematics, which, so we are told, are the clue to the brain's own metadimensions, which in turn, if one sets about it the right way, furnish a clue to the world's.

But still, what power derives from is the plain number sequence.

And of course Mantegna is fully aware of this. The ground plan alone, which he has drawn, says it all. Throughout the centuries perfection in geometry has been reserved for the upper classes. But naturally this is something that this upstart must also have! Even if the wife and children have to live under the stairs, or in the pantry and wine cellar.

(Herein lies the only power I possess, and it is all that I wish for.)

19th August

It is only for Nicolosia's sake that I still send up entreaties to the God who at night throws the stars out into the cold.

21st August

A messenger from Poretta came today. The Cardinal will grace us with a visit. Barbara is wearing black.

24th August

They were here only four hours and were entertained standing up. Lodovico himself went to meet the Cardinal with Federico and two of the grandchildren, Sigismundo and Francesco. Gianfrancesco went along also, if anything to conceal Barbara's resistance to the visit, and has made an excellent report of the meeting in Bondanello.

The Cardinal uttered not a word but presented his father with a letter. Lodovico answered, again not with words, but with a series of gestures and facial expressions, which, at least according to Gianfrancesco's report, were quite comical and completely unintelligible.

Then they set out for the town in silence. Mantegna

35

was on foot with his dogs. The rest on horseback, but Alberti was on the talkative mule which he tried in vain to shut up because it spoiled the impression of solemnity the party wished to make on the livestock that came running up and on the peasants in charge of them.

For the next three hours they stood eating and drinking. Lodovico was happy and felt confirmed in his reputation as father of a pillar of the papal throne. Barbara thought that it was the last time she would see her son.

Incidentally, Mantegna went back to Poretta without so much as a hello to Nicolosia.

8th September

Making nearly daily visits to Nicolosia. Not for love of her. Rather to clarify my hatred for Mantegna. In order to understand how that person has been able to rob me of my love, to make it mute, lonely, and inert. Poor Nicolosia! In you my love is imprisoned, untouchable, and I doubt if I shall ever meet myself again.

21st September

Today Mantegna was called back to Poretta. Nicolosia died suddenly. (She was found this morning near the well in the central courtyard.)

Something inexplicable happened today.

Mantegna invited me to look at his pictures, and I surprised myself by accepting.

If I cared for him I would say it was a successful visit. There is something inside him that quietly defies comprehension, and this is highly stimulating. This insight even allowed me a rare chance to combine civility with candor in a lively, productive manner. But whatever transpires physically, on the surface, will never hide from me the fact that I find his pictures outlandish. On second thought, disgusting is a better word. Even though disgust is not normally something one stops to ponder over.

His obsession, his effects, his transpositions are fundamentally anticlassical, and he stretches the logic so far, that the logical construction breaks apart and disintegrates like so many illusions. "In what the picture relates there should be no loneliness," he remarked several times.

Not a single mention of Nicolosia.

1473

Bartholomeo Manfredi is dead. Not even a month after completing the construction of the astronomical tower clock. Mathematics has lost its freedom of movement.

While Rodolfo was clearing up after Manfredi he found an unfinished letter which looks as if it was to me. All that was written is as follows:

"Dear Marsilio: When you meet Hera, remember she is a pet bird. And if you act as Zeus did and chain her to the clouds, she will certainly give in and succumb. In return she will haunt you for the rest of your life. I have good reason to . . ."

I do not understand it. Rodolfo thinks it is a bachelor joke, from one unmarried man to another, a type of apostolic succession under anti-Zeus. We have been drinking to that. With the papal wine. But I still do not understand it.

Mantegna has finally started on the decoration of the audience chamber. The winter light is the best, he says.

For eight days he has worked on his studies of Nana while I have read to him Poliziano's *Orpheus*.

He says that if Nana had not been a dwarf, she would have been the most beautiful woman in Mantua. "Here in our world," as Mantegna says, "our world of beauty, where beauty is placed under pressure so that we may visibly perceive truth; and where, out of this visible truth, out of this firstborn, a subsequent and more comprehensive beauty may be imagined which at its due time furnishes evidence of the oldest truth, and the deadliest. Which in the hereafter, when beauty has returned to the Land of the Dead, is going to continue its life unseen, as lacunae depicted in all the places where ugliness thrives without our ever perceiving the light she carries within her.

"The hereafter, that is here.

"In this way, for every step we take, the abyss moves with us as sudden visual pockets, as black holes in space, as whiteness in the mind. It is so beautiful it is breathtaking. That I live."

This is the way he can mumble endlessly while he draws the patient Nana.

And still I had to lay Poliziano aside when Orpheus begins to sing for the dead.

26th July

Today the ghost room was finished.

It is Bernardino who calls it the ghost room.

He was seven when Nicolosia died and, with his little sister, he took refuge in the picture of the Madonna to whom Mantegna had given the features of the beloved woman.

They would sit there for hours while Bernardino cried and Gentilia chattered: "When Gentilia comes all the way into the picture, then Gentilia can be together with Mother, and then Mother can lift up Gentilia and kiss her. Lift me up, Bernardino. Lift me up!" And Bernardino lifted her up so she could kiss her mother.

"She tastes like dust. She should be washed. Gentilia will wash her mother with the washcloth!"

"No," said Bernardino, "Mother will do it herself. At night when no one is looking, Mother slips out of the picture and washes herself."

"And comes in and sleeps with me?"

"Yes."

From that moment Gentilia has forgotten her

mother. But Bernardino saw her every night when she came in to sleep and has thereafter been convinced that all portraits are ghosts.

The dedication took place today. The room was called "The Painted Room" in Lodovico's official talk.

Federico wanted permission to call it "The Bridal Chamber," because he would like to see it as a monument to his parents.

"It is not a monument," Barbara said, "it is a dining room."

"Who can get a bite down when all those people are looking at it?" asked Rodolfo.

Then Lodovico pulled the curtain aside and asked all those portrayed on the wall to find themselves among those present. Immediately after, he began to praise the ceiling, which Mantegna has painted to look as though it were open in the middle to the outside; the opening is rimmed by a balustrade over which the female heads and putti look down. And you imagine you can feel the air from the hovering sky wafting down through the "opened" roof.

The Gonzaga family was so enraptured by this pious fraud that they were able to conceal their dismay at seeing Barbara among the female heads on the ceiling; it was youthful and adorned with beads,

41

and placed next to a dark-skinned slave; the face was smiling, almost blissful, at all events lost in a dream, whether beatific or carnal, perhaps both at once and indiscriminately.

Meanwhile the family were further rescued from this awkward discovery thanks to an almost equally awkward episode that occurred when Bernardino suddenly stepped forward and piped up childishly, but with a born artist's confidence, to say that he could relate the thirty-three painted figures on the walls to the corresponding people who, for this occasion, were almost all of them gathered in the room, 26 feet by 26.

There is more life in the paintings than in all of these lively and rapturous spectators who simply put on airs because they are afraid of the pictures' soul which is their own. The pictures are like all great ghosts in Art who calmly and tirelessly wait for their living models to die. All those who have had the chance on this occasion to look at themselves in the light of Art's exegesis have consequently entered into a relationship with Death; and they must each conduct their negotiations with him day by day over the time and place and manner of their dying, and about their measure of anxiety.

The boy's voice, borne on the wings of shame and sorrow as naturally as the bird is lifted up by its wings and the air, carried such persuasiveness, such truth, that for a moment people had a sense of sleepwalking on their way to an abyss which they were convinced would bear them up in eternity's eternity.

Then Mantegna took Bernardino out and the feasting began.

9th August

Mantegna has received an order to remove the portraits of those already deceased. This includes ("for the present," as Bernardino observed, when he heard about it) Manfredi and Alberti.

17th August

Alberti has, with a few rather sarcastic corrections, been turned into Kaiser Frederik III, a complete nonentity who spends most of his time grazing from town to town in Italy, cultivating his passion for pearls and diamonds.

Under no circumstances will Mantegna touch Manfredi. Sure enough the room has been painted according to Lodovico's wishes, but not according to his mind. Indeed it looks as though it was painted in honor of the Gonzaga family, but in reality it is first and foremost Manfredi who is honored, because he is the only one (and Mantegna studiedly says "is" and not "was" the only one), the only one who understands the conversation the room is fated to carry on with itself, because even in his absence, which is the condition of the dead in their wanderings, he is able to follow the invisible lines that lead the thoughts from person to person—and this does not refer exclusively to the thoughts of the painted people, it means all thoughts that exist.

On the other hand, Mantegna has removed his own portrait, which he had placed next to Alberti's. Almost no one, however, will discover he is not there. Anyway, no one has noticed because the shape is still where it has always been. But the eyes have been altered: before, they were so candidly conspiratorial but now, with just a few changes in color, they have become lackluster, wary and dumb. And what before was an expression of natural pride and well-being now looks more like cringing vanity—the look to be found in Christian I of Denmark as he travels around these days extolling his country's greatness and virtue, yes, even its sense of beauty.

He was of course treated in accordance with his own self-image when he visited Mantua in March. But nobody made a secret of the whole thing's being a delusion. In this way, the Danish king came to be the centerpiece of an exaggerated charade, which the children especially knew how to appreciate. "It is just a game we play," they cried, and they applauded Christian I, the fairy-tale king from a faraway, inaccessible, wonderful country where naturally no people could live, but that made it all the better to dream about and long for. And to tell stories about.

About a country, where Cold and Dark argued over who was the stronger while the inhabitants slept. Their sleep was not safe and sound, not a good sleep, not an ordinary night's sleep that empties the body of sadness and sorrow. No, their sleep was a sick and deathlike torpor, filled with all kinds of needs they could not identify, so it did not matter how much they ate, they never became replete, and no matter how much they knew, they never became clever, and no matter how much they made love, they never became warmer. Therefore in the end, they stopped touching each other and spent all their time mocking each other until the last person, who believed he knew something, learned to keep it to himself. Until then everyone was the same, shoveling food into their heads without noticing what it was they were eating. Without seeing.

"It is just something we play," said the children, and dreamed of melting the heart of the foreign princess and giving her apples, oranges, and a free-ranging imagination, instead of porridge and melancholy.

(The Land of the Dead is the Prince's utopia. On the other hand, it is never freedom we should be granting the princess but the right and opportunity to explain her life with passion, as a part of the unapproachable freedom against which our world order lays its ingenious schemes.

No doubt about it. This world order is wrong. Because it is explained and interpreted wrongly. Because we think and feel wrongly. Because we think that on the reverse side of this order chaos rules. And because this order thus becomes enmeshed with chaos, it falls prey to weariness, exploitation, apathy.

What we ought to think is that on the reverse side of this order freedom rules, and it is with this freedom that we ought to conduct our conversations about the interpretation of life among people and in the world.

By entering into our hearts under the rule of chaos and seeing there generation after generation destroyed under the burden of despair, we could reach the point of entering our hearts in freedom and seeing one human life after the next winning through to the land of the living—a land that the poets in the future will celebrate more beautifully and deeply than they have previously sung about the Land of the Dead.

The Land of the Dead is the Prince's utopia because he believes in chaos. The day we, in our ordinary human lives, believe in freedom, the realm of the living will be all the world's utopia. Our world order can be changed only when we no longer fear chaos, but have confidence in the reign of freedom.)

18th August

Again tonight I saw Nicolosia stepping towards my bed with closed eyes, as an exile who had sworn that she would never see her exile.

12th September

I shall soon turn fifty, and I am amazed to see that before this happens I may be calling myself Mantegna's confidant. Perhaps even his only confidant, next to Bernardino of course.

In contrast, I have lost all ambition in my relationship to Lodovico, and my accounts of the wine from the Capitol were suspended a long time ago. I drink it at last in peace of mind, all the more so because a while ago it suddenly improved. Many years ago we spoke about miracles, and in our admiration for Lodovico we even thought that he at his moment of death would invoke these miracles and give us an unforgettable wake, but now when chance outruns him and all the rest of us, we have hardly noticed what has happened. Nobody has in any case noticed when it happened, and everyone has looked at the transformation as something completely natural (and therefore inexplicable).

Mantegna says, because we have so faithfully drunk the sour wine, it now rewards us with its sweetness. Because we have forgotten about our stubborn expectations of the impossible, we are now rewarded with the most impossible of all, an indulgent life without the burden of shame that gratitude imposes.

13th September

What I really wanted to tell about being in Mantegna's confidence is that we regularly meet in "The Ghost Room" where we devote ourselves to the study of psychological space and to speculating on how the individual finds himself in (or puts up with) others, and how he finds others in himself, and calls this ceaseless artistic movement the State.

"If the State can be a work of art," Mantegna says, "then the work of art can just as well be a state."

The late Alberti insisted throughout his life that the State ought to be a work of art. He himself was as far from implementing his vision as anyone else. Particularly in his last years he frightened his associates out of their wits, and eventually, when everybody had abandoned him, he died in conversation with his mule. They say that the last words Alberti whispered in the stubborn creature's ear were, "The State is me." And the mule answered, "No, the State is us."

"Yes, the mule was right," Mantegna said, "for it would be pointless to dream about freedom unless we include Alberti and the mule in the same state. And the State does not have to be an evil if all its members were subjected to all its members—not by making the individual subject to the judgment of the majority but by ensuring that all of us, each as an individual, are made responsible for the individual's crime no matter in which person this crime was manifested.

"If the mule was stupid then so was Alberti. If Alberti was a genius then the mule was surely in his way one as well. Although no one can ever be a universal genius like Alberti without at the same time being stupid."

1478

Lodovico is dead.

After his body was laid out, he was placed in "The Ghost Room," where Pico, whom chance brought here yesterday, gave a short oration. A traditional speech, but nevertheless I found in it a stimulating message and an authentic comfort.

"Not until people become God does God really exist. This is why we so seldom get a sense of that belief which so graciously accompanies us all our life!"

The music was unfortunately very poor. The musicians had all been lent out to Ferrara, and when they were called home in haste they were all so drunk that they laughed at the very mention of Lodovico's name.

All we could procure were two of Mantegna's craftsmen who gave a passable performance on the zither and the krummhorn.

1st December

Today I did something unusual. I took the seven times seventeen peacock feathers which the women had held in continuous motion over Lodovico's corpse in a desperate attempt to revive him. When it became apparent that he had already been dead a long time and they, in their blind fury, wanted to tear the feathers to bits, I called them to order, gathered up the feathers, and put them away. I reasonably explained to the incredulous women that they would certainly find plenty more occasions to make use of these as we are all gradually getting older. Since then they have been lying on my table.

But today I took them, wrapped them in a cloth, and walked softly in the twilight to Nicolosia's grave, where I spread them out as seven wonderful peacock tails held in place by some pebbles I found in the vicinity. Then I went home.

And here I sit and wait. Not for death, nor for life, but for a motion I have repressed in myself for a long time. For tears that can make the paradise garden bloom again. Differently. Not overwhelming, as the physical world, but overwhelmed as a world of creativity.

I have been embittered and old since my youth. In a split second I have been a murderer; in a split second I have nearly been God; I have cultivated the negation of joy, and people have thought me a sphinx; I have cultivated the denial of happiness, and have treated myself as a machine; I have cultivated the negation of life, and have been like a monk against the world in all its multiplicity. I have nibbled at a tiny bit, the rest I have recklessly thrown away.

Now when the regrets still do not come …

1492

24th July

Andrea held a reception today in the still unfinished house. He has lived there since the autumn of '90 when he returned from Rome. But only today was the inscription put in place: "Here on this spot in the world Andrea Mantegna continued to build his house."

Today it is exactly one year since I moved in with the little that belonged to me, mostly these manuscripts and a couple of good pieces of furniture that had belonged to my father, plus my private wine cellar which, on that occasion, was enlarged by the rest of the papal wine from 1444.

When Francesco and Isabella moved in, every corner of the castle was inspected. The wine jars were also found, but when Isabella learned that they were never put to their intended use, she immediately required that they part with them lest they remind her of the moment — remote, it is to be hoped — when her husband would die. Oh well, these newly wed children build their nest as if it is to last forever.

Tonight we took the wine out after the guests from the reception had left. Then we held a commemoration, just the two of us, for all who had died. For Lodovico, Barbara, Federico, and Alberti. For the gardener Baldassare and for Manfredi. For our parents and for many others we have known, separately or together, as children, as youths, or until recently. For Vittorini da Feltre, for Pizzolo, for Samuele da Tradate, and for Luca Fancelli. For Pico della Mirandola, who died last year, and last but not least, for our good doctor Gherardo da Verona, who fought so passionately for Bernardino's life that time in 1480.

For Bernardino. Who daily brings us together.

We never mention Nicolosia.

10th November

It is very likely that the house will never be finished.

The plan has been to have an arched dome over the atrium, but Andrea has at last given up the project and instead let someone carve a marble basin to collect rainwater and snow.

Of the fifteen rooms, only a couple are completed, with walls and doors. The housekeeper lives in one of these rooms. And the other, for the most part, is left empty. In the rest of the house there are only hints where one has to imagine boundaries for the individual rooms, sometimes with unfinished brick-work, sometimes with a pair of columns, but in most cases, with a pile of sculptures, antiques, and plants.

The plants grow almost better here indoors than outside. During the summer they press their way in through the outer wall of the garden unrestrictedly, seeking shade and coolness from the whitewashed room.

All the same, Mantegna works tirelessly on this artistic building and spends all of what he owns on marble, on color samples, on firing and glazing, on fusing and chasing, and on the cleverest and most expressive artisans. This patience costs him dearly.

I am not saying that I hope the house is never finished. I am not saying that, but deep down, it is exactly what I hope for. I am attracted to the ill-defined transitions between Art and Nature, and when I see the way the young apprentices who come here to learn drawing and perspective fare better in depicting the leafy vines that wind around the base of a column than they do with the column itself, then I am deeply delighted. And if I see them mistake flowers and fruit for different sorts of colored stones, I am more delighted than ever. Then I see how strong the physical world is when it reveals itself obliquely to artists' educated perceptions.

As Andrea said the last time we visited "The Ghost Room": "Of us (artists) there will be nothing left, but our fellow human beings will speak through our pictures. Who has painted these people? Whose art is it to send forth this foolish, divine gaze into eternity, as if it were an apple to be eaten? It is Paolina's, not mine. It is Barberina's and Nana's, not mine. It is the children's. All of the children who survive us, their curiosity outstripping us in the grown-ups' questions about mortality."

1506

Andrea Mantegna is dead.

I am sitting beside the bed and understand nothing. Never, even as a child, have I felt such love, so happy and free.

When I told him a while ago that it was I who murdered Nicolosia, all he answered was, he had known all along. That he thought the best he could do in his sorrow was to turn directly to me and keep me close to him, because chance had bound me to his person.

Then finally resentment came out. Penitence. Poor Nicolosia whom I sacrificed in order to ruin my own life.

And so I am sitting here and waiting. Here, on this spot in the world Marsilio Andreasi goes on sitting and waiting.

While the paradise garden blooms as it did the first time we saw each other: Marsilio and Nicolosia, Nicolosia and Andrea, Andrea and Marsilio, and all the seven times seventeen peacock eyes, which form the complete sorrow.

II

THE PEACOCKS' SECRET

1

They found an old washtub down by the river and dragged it up to the courtyard. There they played as if it were a carriage that carried them up into the mountains or out to sea. Then and there they had the world at their feet, and no one ever caught them any more longing for what could not be had. They were human beings — that much they knew — and although they were barely three or four years old, they worked every day from dawn to dusk with much more energy than they would summon later in life to make the world immortal.

One evening Nana sat in the high grass over near the south wall and cried. She cried because she was a dwarf. She cried because her mouth, now that both she and her lover had turned sixteen, could no longer reach up to his mouth. When she reached up, her mouth came only to the middle of his thigh and although she might perhaps find another, shorter man to love if she looked for one, he would surely be only that much shorter so that her mouth reached his loins instead. Perhaps he would be so strong he could lift her up so that her mouth could meet his, but at the same time her sex would only touch his chest. It would not even reach as far down as his navel. Never again, in all the dreadfully long life that towered up before her, would she be at one with the world.

But the gardener Baldassare, who had seen her sorrow, went to her with his youngest and most beautiful son, nine-year-old Piero.

"You're sitting on the tub we need to use," he said. "Get up and help us." Then he tightened the iron band firmly around the tub, forced it up, and asked Piero and Nana to carry it.

"We're going into the secret garden," he said.

Through an underground passage they came to a courtyard that was surrounded by walls, without a single opening, neither door nor window, to be seen.

Here they filled the tub with dirt and watered it well.

"We're going to plant wedding flowers," said Baldassare.

"For me," whispered Nana.

"Yes, and Piero shall water them and take care of them until your wedding day."

"What are wedding flowers?" asked Piero.

"They are oranges," said his father, "like those you usually steal."

"And now I'll get some that are only mine . . . which other people can steal."

"Not if you take good care of them."

"You can bet I'll take good care of them," said Piero. And when they were leaving he gave Nana a kiss on the forehead, as he was already a little bit taller than she was.

The orange tree is an evergreen and bears blossoms all the time. If the blossoms flourish, then the tree bears fruit all the time as well. Because of this characteristic merging of different stages in the tree's life, it has always been a symbol of purity, chastity, and fertility all at the same time. And therefore precisely the symbol of eternal love.

Being the practical people they were, Piero and Nana understood this secret, but never mentioned it.

Piero took care of the plant all summer and winter, and ate its fruit nearly before it was ripe. In this way the blooming was hastened and the tree soon grew tall.

There were enough blossoms for a crown and for garlands to cover all of her radiant little person from head to foot. They danced around the plucked tree in the tub in the secret garden which, this morning, was opened for everyone. The sun and the wine made all the guests feverish, but it was not until the evening, when the chill descended on the enclosed courtyard, that they noticed how they were feeling. Only half of the guests attended the concluding portion of the ceremony, shivering and snuggling up to each other like young birds who sense from the change in feather movements that a storm is on the way.

The newly married couple picked the last two fruits from the disfigured tree. Nana peeled one of them and shared it with Piero. Piero put the other one under his shirt. In great haste the young couple was bundled into the house Gonzaga had bestowed upon his daughter.

The second orange was never eaten. Piero took it, poked his love's name with cloves into its peel, and hung it, without anyone seeing, in the sooty chimney.

The wedding crown was never thrown away. For some, this was out of kindness. For others, this was out of spite that they neglected to tell Nana how important it was that the flowers be destroyed before the end of the first month of marriage unless one actually wanted the marriage to be childless.

Piero was absorbed in his own affairs; he was a practical man who was fond of domestic tranquility and

peaceful meals. Therefore he allowed Nana to lie
and play on his stomach when they were in bed, like
a little child who finds warmth and zest with her
mother. Sometimes he let her ride on his lap until
she screamed with delight and flew up to his mouth
and kissed him.

2

For as long as anyone in Mantua could remember, never had there been a marriage between such a mismatched couple. It was said that he was as handsome as she was rich. That it was she who was passionate while he was cold. And that it was he who was sensible while she was shameless, irritable, and cowardly. Most of what people said was accurate of course. But this last thing appeared to be so wrong that when people finally realized the truth they became only the more incredulous and set in their beliefs.

At that strange wedding there was a woman present with such an indeterminable appearance, it was difficult to guess her age.

Apparently no one knew her name, so she was called the woman with the white headband, an ornament she wore across an arrow-straight middle parting with the sides stuck down through her hair. The hair was coiled up like two big puffs at her ears. She wore a white dress that looked as if it might have been made for a wedding that never happened.

In the way that sisters can sometimes be tart and

prudish, other times sweet and banal, and, on rare occasions, starry-eyed and distant, this woman was a sister in precisely this way. But whose sister she was, nobody knew.

On the day of the wedding, while the guests, during the siesta, looked for shade under the little trees of the secret garden or under the trellis with its climbing roses, this woman drifted around from group to group, but spoke to no one.

Because of her erect posture and sad, indulgent smile, many believed she was an unknown sister, possibly only a half sister, of Lodovico Gonzaga's. But when he treated her distantly, although without hostility, three of the more curious women decided to question Marsilio about her. No, he did not know her, he said, he had not sent her an invitation. Maybe there was something familiar about her, but this was all he could say: there were so many guests, invited and uninvited, and as you know, this is not an occasion when we wish to encroach upon the wedding's basic principle of open hospitality. The marriage should be a house where the door stands open, not a jail. That of course implies a risk, but without danger there is no marriage, only a house with occupants, furniture, and kitchen utensils.

The three women of course already knew that

Marsilio was ill-tempered and arrogant, because he had never married, and therefore they had no hope of understanding either him or marriage or anything at all. They were driven by boredom to keep looking for riddles everywhere, not so much in order to solve them, as to spread them about as rumors, true or false, which would increase the number of riddles. "It is always such a pity to miss something," they said to each other. And so they flung themselves back into their pursuit of the woman with the white headband.

As far as it is known, they never got into a conversation with her—the remarkable thing is that she neither made up to the men, nor treated the women to sarcastic comments. When she joined a group she would hang back at the edge and listen, but as soon as one person or another signified, perhaps with a look, that he or she was going to address her, she would lower her eyes or slip away as imperceptibly as possible to the next group. After a while it was clear to nearly everyone that she apparently wished to pass unnoticed. Most people thought she was shy about being an old maid but at the same time was too clever to believe she could do anything about it. But if she had no hope of finding a man, said the three curious women, then why in the world had she come?

Certainly a woman who had not been able to get herself either a man or a child had willfully jeopardized her standing, and no matter which social position she had been born into, she had violated the image of a real woman so that she could only be considered an outcast, a person who conveyed no symbolic value whatsoever.

If, with such a background, she still had the energy to change her situation, she could do it in only one way: she could turn herself into an enigma.

Obviously she could become neither a demon nor an angel, since these revered manifestations were reserved for masculine enigmas. Either she could become a witch, if she was strong-willed and had an ugly or lascivious appearance, or she could become a saint, if she had a gentle disposition and an aura of holiness, which she could display and promote wisely until the Church sanctioned her refined hysteria.

This sort of respect and inviolability was their only recourse, but few are those women who achieve it. The road is long and chancy and the danger of death lurks at every corner. Besides, most women in this unfortunate situation preferred to take this detour on the road to death, shorter or longer as it might be, rather than opt for suicide, the choice for women of a more nebulous cast of mind, if their guiding spirits demanded an immediate change in their condition.

For the woman with the white headband apparently none of these solutions became necessary. It was decided on the afternoon that she spent in the wedding garden that she should be called history's first feminine angel. How this actually came about is a longer story, which only a few of the guests, at a much later time, were to be lucky enough to learn. That strange day when they were still in ignorance, they believed in anything and everything that left them feeling sated with pleasure.

And at around six o'clock they had seen this woman with two other women dressed in white whom they had not noticed earlier at the party; they saw them with their own eyes, pulling Nana to one side while their figures were bathed in a light that seemed almost celestial. They bent over her with such an air of unapproachable authority and grace as to paralyze wicked tongues and move the virtuous to utter an overawed hallelujah, like birds giving tongue in the silence of dawn.

When a little later Nana was asked to describe what occurred and what the ladies had said, she blushed deeply and gave evasive answers. She cried the whole time even as she was smiling and looking happier than any ordinary bride should, dwarf though she was, so they did not press her. Immediately after this incident the three strange women vanished, which only strengthened the guests' impression that a revelation had occurred.

The only one who had had a more down-to-earth impression of the three women was Mantegna, who had drawn all three of them in many different versions, especially the first woman with the white headband.

His sketch pad showed clearly, however, that one of the pair who had made their sudden appearance looked identical to the first lady, except that a small measure of doubt lingered round the mouth, which had only been hinted at in one of Mantegna's drawings. But otherwise they were indeed identical — the same headbands, the same buckles, their indeterminate character, their deportment that suggested unmarried, childless women. The second woman was depicted with wavy hair down her back, and she looked so much younger. As many had correctly observed, she held a little book open in her right hand. Seeing her like this, in Mantegna's drawings, detached from the others, one began to wonder whether she was in fact a woman at all.

*

To all this visible evidence Mantegna could add a verbal testimony: when questioned directly, the first woman in the white headband had said that she was the Pope's sister. No one, however, placed much reliance on this claim. It was felt that an angel's word should not be taken as literally as a sister's.

3

Two of the women in the white headbands who were taken for angels that afternoon could nonetheless claim something as normal as an odd childhood.

They were born in Basel. Their mother was carried off by the plague when they were very young and their father, who served in the garrison on the northern frontier, could think of nothing better to do for the twin sisters than to apply to place them in Cardinal Capranica's household which, at that time, during the synod in Basel, had opened its doors to all sorts of unfortunates.

The responsibility for the girls' well-being now devolved upon Capranica's secretary, the ingenious and practical Piccolomini, and this he fulfilled with great imagination and cheerfulness. Every evening, once the Cardinal had retired after dinner, the beggars were invited in to eat the plentiful leftovers. In this company the girls were passed from hand to hand and were so happy and playful as they had their meal that for a while their elders would forget the hunger and rough living that were once more to be their lot when the synod was over.

The sisters were both named Maria. No one knew what name they had been given by their parents, though each quite possibly would have had a name of her own. People tried every possible way to tell them apart.

Here in Cardinal Capranica's retinue it was different. Enea Silvio Piccolomini was a man of democratic ideas, under the impetus of which people took pride in recognizing the girls as two persons in one being. True enough, this one being moved in two separate parts, but since their movements were so perfectly coordinated, no importance at all could be attached to this bisection. Thus it was that the two little girls became a symbol of humankind's inevitable unity, and it was generally considered that this unity could best be promoted by emphasizing its external features. Of course not everyone can be given the same appearance, but they can all be accorded the same rights and opportunities, the same chance of happiness.

What either Maria might have thought or felt about it is a question nobody asked.

Piccolomini was so convinced about the naturalness of his thoughts that he tied his fate ever closer to this straightforward symbol, which he, thanks to Cardinal Capranica's capriciousness, had received in his charge.

But symbols that one has watched grow up, symbols that one had a hand in creating, will tend to be different from those that have become what they are as a result of several generations of effort.

So it was that in 1447, when Piccolomini was appointed Bishop of Trieste, he had already been married for a long time to both the Maria sisters. Three years later, when the family was moved to Siena, the Bishop's wives bore him, within an interval of a few minutes, a son and a daughter. He could hardly confess to anyone he had been hoping to see twins, four baby daughters to replace the pair he had taken in marriage, but he quickly recovered his composure and took the necessary precautions to straighten out his symbolic idea. The newborn son was immediately sent out to a wet nurse, while the daughter was raised up and exalted as the perfect image of human reconciliation, be it with fellow human beings as also between Man and God.

To which end, the girl was called Lucia and was brought up exactly as if she were a boy.

The Maria sisters proved to be living instruments of human reconciliation day by day throughout their lives. If Piccolomini had wanted to prove himself, he did so in the realization of his transcendental ambition.

Since in his own arrangements the action always followed hard on the heels of the thought, Piccolomini became a cardinal in '55 and in '58 made his entry into Rome as Pope Pius II; in his suite were his wives, clad in white, and Lucia similarly dressed in white, and mounted on a dapple-gray horse with a sky-blue harness.

This child, truly a creature of wonder, created a greater sensation than any Pope, and Piccolomini was proud of his family and happy about the reception they had been accorded.

Even though most people knew better, it was decided that the three women should from now on be presented as the Pope's sisters. Officially it was determined that inside the papal residence they were to conduct themselves as men in a man's world. They were not supposed to change sex but, aside from this, they were in every way to be regarded as men and should, as far as it was possible, receive an education, pass the necessary tests, and remain at the Pope's disposal for special assignments.

Of course this was all on the condition that such norms should prove compatible with the Pope's wish for a private life.

Yes, he wished for a private life. But as to whether it

should be lived in the company of the Maria sisters, he was as yet undecided. Over the years he had cultivated a longstanding acquaintance with many women, and he wondered what effect it would have on them if he now returned to them as Pope.

It is said he summoned the Congress in Mantua in 1459 in order to incite the indolent princes against the Turks. Certainly this was his sincere intention, but it was an intention he settled upon first and foremost because it was consistent with two of his most urgent plans. The first was Piccolomini's wish to see the son he had put out to nurse immediately after birth, and whom he knew he could find at the home of Baldassare Mancinelli, the devout gardener and nature lover. Second, he wanted once more to meet and love Lodovico Gonzaga's wife — she was the woman who had made the deepest impression on him. This was not only because she had loved him so naturally, calling neither heaven nor hell to witness, but equally as much because of her egalitarian ideas — humanistic rather than God-centered. This had been the strongest motivating force in his fight, first against the Pope, then against the Antipope, and lastly against the competing cardinals.

The boy disappointed him. Maybe this was because he had expected to find in him the face of one of the

Marias, but instead found his own, so exactly copied that the mere sight of it alarmed him. The gardener had called the boy Piero after his grandfather, and he never had grounds to complain because the boy was through and through as sensible as anyone could wish and had skills that would surely take him far.

Pius II said nothing, but reflected on the lively, intractable child he himself had been.

Most possibly the damage done could never be repaired, but by arranging a really good match for his son he could at least give him the opportunity to extend himself, even if it turned out that he didn't have the skills for it.

It was that afternoon that Baldassare and Piero had gone to visit the tearful Nana. At that point the wedding day had been already determined for nine years later, the 23rd of May 1468.

4

Just as Nana was being dressed for her wedding the peacocks arrived. Because of the vine leaves two of the birds may have thought she was a tree, for they flew up and sat on her shoulders and managed to eat several of the crown's juicy leaves before Marsilio and his helper chased them off.

The birds, for the time being, were placed in what was later called "The Ghost Room," where Mantegna had plans to paint a spreading peacock tail as the frame around each volute of the ceiling. It was for this purpose the birds were purchased, although they were never used for it. The only peacock Mantegna got into his mural was without a tail.

The tail was hidden behind a balustrade which he had painted in such a way as to leave the open sky showing through the ceiling. There under the blue-painted sky the peacock came to roost, eternally stretching its neck out towards the butterfly in the center of the sky.

But when the day arrived, the peacock cried incessantly with the six others and fanned out its tail feathers, especially adapted for this purpose, in order to win a suitable portion of "The Ghost Room" which it could call its own.

Only when Nana stole away from her wedding and spoke with the seven bird guests did a stillness fall over them and they swept the floor with their peacock-tail trains and cackled like barnyard fowls.

Of course that May day these peacocks were the object of countless conflicting auguries. Nonetheless, for the moment this day belonged to the angels. These human birds, nonexistent though they might be, impressed the guests with their concentrated lightness, their delicate femininity, and their defiance of death, and for a long time after Piero and Nana's wedding, when women complained about their earthbound fate, it seemed almost right and proper that they should.

Only from Nana was there never a whisper of complaint to be heard, for all that she was sad that Piero was not willing ever to talk with her intimately about life and death, about dreams for the future. He tended to roam about the countryside beyond the river; but when he was at home, he was easy enough as a companion; he ate her food, slept in her bed and let her play on his lap.

She found nothing strange in his inability to settle straight into a peaceful domestic routine or to decide on a specific employment. What did puzzle her was why he returned at all each evening and behaved just as if he had been anybody else.

Had the angels not told her that she could expect something out of the ordinary? They had told her that Piero was the Pope's son and as such he was predestined for something great through her. Even though time passed and nothing happened, she was quite comfortable with her expectations. All her life she had been hoping for a miracle, that God would let her grow and become a human being like others. Now, once Piero had come into her life, she felt that such a sudden development was more imminent than ever before.

Most of the day, and during the summer in the evening as well, as she waited for her dreamy Piero to come home, she sat and read "The Angels' Book," as she called it, because she had been given it as a present from the youngest of the angels, the one who had looked at Piero with such longing that for a moment Nana had feared the worst.

But this book really was about the worst. Maybe that is why she read it over and over again in an attempt to search through the worst and find the hidden meaning, the ultimate purpose of life, the very thing which she longed to discuss with her beloved Piero when she lay awake at night moping over their nice, ineffectual household.

The book had been written by Piero's father seven or eight years before the boy was born. It was impossible to imagine that it was written by any ordinary father, but of course it was far more impossible to imagine it being written by a Pope—unless it was simply an enigma, and Nana was determined to crack it.

The book was called *De Duobus Amantibus Historia*, the story of two lovers, and was about Eurealus and Lucretia and their elated despair. In 1432 Eurealus comes to Siena as one of the many noblemen in Kaiser Sigismund's retinue, and there he falls at once so deeply in love with Lucretia that he is quite simply unable to respect her marriage to the wealthy Menelaus.

His passion is promptly reciprocated, but it is only after numerous love letters and sundry obstacles that the lovers eventually succeed in uniting in the bed that awaits them.

However, in order to get Menelaus to leave his town and abandon his pursuits, they find it necessary to contrive a small border war; and for Eurealus to put up with living disguised as a servant if he is to partake of the only life that he craves—Lucretia's.

This lasts for one year; then the Kaiser sweeps off northwards with his retinue, Love's bondsman leaves Siena, and Eurealus's devoted mistress dies of grief.

Menelaus returns to a corpse that is more visibly Lucretia than she had been whilst still alive.

In the back of the book in a lined leather pocket Nana found about a dozen folded pages of poetry which she could only decipher with the greatest difficulty.

One of these poems was about angels in the fire of earthly feelings; about an angel who burned with a light so intensely white there was hardly any ash from the fire and therefore nothing with which to fertilize the fields and humankind, although possibly there was enough for the invisible plants in the garden of paradise—plants that presumably have had to wait an eternity to obtain a definitive ruling on the question of their pictorial effect.

Another poem, and the one Nana was most fond of, was called "Song to My Peacock," and even though it was not a proper song because it was filled with complex thoughts, she was very fond of singing it as she fed the peacocks. It could not be said that her voice gave the song wings, rather it formed a cozy little nest in which two never fully incubated eggs — irascibility and love — lay side by side and waited. The peacocks listened quietly and once in a while there came a cry from their songless throats:

> *How beautiful to pull the sky around on a string*
> *and tug it open for all those who stand staring.*
>
> *What was my peacock without its gaudy train?*
> *How I love these silly birds so big and sly*
> *dragging around the whole celestial plain,*
> *revealing what they ought to hide,*
> *that the sky is an underground cave deep and wide*
> *at the bottom of an even bigger land that's spinning.*
> *How beautiful to pull the sky around on a string.*
>
> *It spreads its tail for anyone to behold*
> *who seems childish in the peacock's eyes,*
> *while furling it for those who've grown old*
> *and take no pleasure in the world's exquisite lies.*
> *Truth's many hours continue naked as they fly*
> *through life and like a bewailing chorus they sing.*
> *How beautiful to pull the sky around on a string.*
>
> *So hard to coax the truth from ice,*
> *so hard to hatch from earthly cold,*
> *dragging your beauty around like a scythe,*
> *dreaming of heads that have to roll*
> *until patterns of meaning start to unfold.*

Be meaningless and your nature's king!
How beautiful to pull the sky around on a string!

That one cannot is as obvious as it seems
and thus we feel the greatest ease
when the sky shakes then we ourselves must laugh and beam,
blowing all explanations away with the breeze.
The universe offers a crutch that we seize
and on it alone we leave our markings.

How beautiful to pull the sky around on a string
listening to the peacock's hoarse words ring.

5

Then one day Piero was gone, and Nana warmed up the meal each hour and cried as silently as the water that for centuries seeps through the mountain rocks.

But she did not complain, and when the others asked after Piero, she covered up his absence with all possible excuses and explanations. He was probably hunting for hare or he had gone to Florence to buy jewelry or new doormats, or he had taken up with a party of artists and gone with them to the mountains in search of inspiration.

Most people thought that he had gone to Venice or Milan to seek excitement and to perish in the unknown. What a young peasant!

But Nana knew better. Either he had sought refuge with his sister Lucia and her openhearted love, without knowing who she was, or else he had entered a religious order to follow in his father's footsteps. The latter was unquestionably the less painful choice and, as soon as she received word from him, she would take up residence close by and support and encourage him in his new life.

But word never came.

*

One year passed, and people began to consider Piero lost to this world or, in any case, to Mantua, and when at last Nana bore a son, one thought immediately that he was most likely the work of the angels and decided to rejoice in it. Nana said nothing, but felt a little lonely now and then when she rocked the sleeping cherub.

What the old women whispered was neither good nor evil. In fact, it is an ill wind that blows nobody good, and it could all have easily gone much worse when you considered that the bridal wreath was never thrown away, but lay withering in the chest along with the bedding and the embroidered covers. All things considered, it verged on the miraculous that the little Gonzaga dwarf had conceived a child to nurse. She could probably manage without her husband. He was just the gardener's son, and in the Gonzaga family they have always been so brimming with ideas and discussed politics and played cards in the master's vineyard. No, it was just as well she got rid of him! And the fact is, she had grown into a little tiny bit of a beauty once she was on her own and no longer had to cudgel her brains over what she was going to make for dinner. Nana herself never breathed a word to anyone about Piero, only to the peacocks that she loved to be with at midday when everything was so

89

quiet she could clarify her thoughts and tell them to the clucking birds.

One day she was caught deep in conversation with them by her mother, who had lain in wait and who had heard her mention Piero as being the son of Pius II.

Barbara was furious, and Nana was immediately brought in to be questioned about it.

Here she told everything that she knew, which was more or less what the angels had said in the revelation at the wedding. She ended by explaining that the angels had forced her to make a promise she could not understand, to reveal nothing of what they had told her. Now of course she regretted she had kept that promise for so long, but she had never stopped to ponder what it could mean.

And when now and then she had felt the urge to share the secret with her mother, it had been because she thought that it would please her and serve to make her still more devout.

Now Barbara no longer knew if she should laugh or cry, but in any case, the time had come when Nana ought to hear all of her story. And Duchess Barbara told it:

"It was all so long ago that it seems like a story that never happened, a story I once read, about a number of people I barely knew, then forgot as I was reading. But it has actually happened.

"It was in 1442 when Federico was a baby and his life was the most wonderful one that has ever been lived on earth — that was how I felt. At that time Frederik III came to Mantua and his retinue broke over the town like a wave, lifting us up and throwing us down again on the surface of the water that had risen in a flood tide.

"At the crest of this wave was a man my own age. The moment his eyes met mine he signaled silently that he loved me, and that this love had to come to fruition. And it did.

"Of course, although we exchanged letters and poems, I hesitated, but the fact is, not much time passed before I was thinking more about this foreign lover than I did about my husband Lodovico; yes, I even forgot about little Federico for hours on end. There was no preventing it.

"My lover was apparently aware of all this from the start. From the very first day, amidst the confusion surrounding the plans to accommodate the visitors, he had made himself invisible, so he was never introduced in his real person but adopted the guise of a servant so as to gain free access into our house day and night.

"Nevertheless, I could not receive him as long as

Lodovico was in Mantua, but, as always, he found a solution, and quickly fomented a conflict on our northern frontier which Lodovico and his liege men had to take care of.

"During this interval we lived happily together in a union which in every respect developed and deepened even after Lodovico had returned, so much so that eventually I was on the point of asking Lodovico for a divorce. But suddenly one morning my faithful servant was gone and even if I had had the courage, I would never have found the energy to track him down because a month later you were born, and we called you Nana.

"You were so little and wrinkled and shriveled, it defied understanding, and from day to day it was a wonder to me how you survived at all. But after fourteen days you smiled, and very quickly your face showed such a quantity of messages and expressions that we realized your mind had begun to develop at such an unbelievable speed that the body could not possibly keep up.

"Lodovico was inconsolable when our doctors confirmed that you were a dwarf and gave it as their opinion that the fault lay with him. As a youth Lodovico was extremely shy because he had always stayed in the shadow of Carlo. When for years and years you have to look up to a brother who is younger than you, then it takes you a long time to accept yourself. If you ever do.

"In any case I have never told him — that he was not to blame."

"That I am a dwarf," said Nana, "is my own fault."

"No, it can only be mine," said Barbara. "Or the Pope's."

"The Pope's?"

"Yes, your father's name is Pius II."

"Piero's father?"

"Yes, Enea Silvio Piccolomini, father to quite a few children, and he has apparently done all he could do to marry them off to each other."

"What a sublime idea! Maybe it was his plan to make a better world," said Nana.

"You always side with your father, no matter what his name is. Be happy that his son left before you had children together," said Barbara firmly. And there was an end to the discussion.

Nana held her peace, but the following year she bore two more little angels, whom the old women of Mantua praised as the most beautiful boys they had ever seen. One of them had thick blond hair and looked like a hero. The other one had dark hair and busily turned thoughts over in his mind even as he slept.

Nana also pondered. While the boys slept, she speculated on the mysteries of life and tried to make plans to foster them as they should be.

"All that I think and say happens!" This is probably the way her father lived. Perhaps this was what is called faith. Perhaps he had written his story about Lucretia and Eurealus in order to pluck up the courage to enact it in his own person.

Of course it was necessary to give the story a different ending. Lucretia died, but it was the type of effect that a storyteller necessarily has to turn to, so as to create in the reader such a heightened terror that he would take everything else in the story on trust.

In reality the story had a different ending. Barbara refused to die as in the conclusion to Piccolomini's story. Perhaps it was not finished at all. Perhaps it was she, Nana, who would in due course reveal the ending or signal it somewhere in that future she too was never going to see.

6

Nana might be excused for entertaining the long-held hope of turning the family curse into a blessing and undergoing the experience along with everybody else in the world.

She knew nothing of how Piccolomini's proposals had been thwarted by reality, nor did she know how he had made a second attempt to realize his Lucretia story.

He had arrived for the Congress in Mantua borne by the twelve bastards from Este. Like a white spring cloud of feathers, silk, and flowers they whirled in through the town, and it looked as though the horses had wings. In any case, there were several who thought they had heard Pope Pius II mumbling to himself: "Within the storm the storm is a cloud that stands still."

Those first days, he had carefully avoided Barbara and behaved as though he intended to forget their shared past, to regard it as a sinful incident.

He had not much luck in his efforts to stir up the

European princes to launch another crusade against the Turks. Most of them did not ever appear in Mantua and, in fact, did not even send representatives. Only a few of the Italian princely houses gave a reluctant assent, among them Gonzaga, and he did so merely because as host he felt he could not decently refuse. Most of them refused on the excuse that the Pope's cardinals, without exception, had remained in Rome. They rejected all idea of war against the taciturn Turkish sultan.

But Pius II continued, as was his nature, to consider the Congress in Mantua as a victory, first and foremost because Lodovico set off the moment the holy war was officially declared on the 14th of January 1460, even though his astrologers had advised him against doing so. This was not so much on the grounds of what they had read in the stars, as of what they had read in old Piccolomini's surreptitious glances at Barbara.

But their anxiety was groundless, for when Piccolomini declared that he was ready once again to be Duchess Barbara's servant, even dressed as a pope, he was met with such a solemn coolness that deep down he had to admit the Congress in Mantua would never lead to victory.

With the look of one who had compassed his own defeat he left Mantua, and determined to die in order to improve the story of his life now that he felt he no longer could embellish it by living.

When he felt the time had come, the 14th of June 1464, he took leave of the Church and the City. Four days later the dying Pope was sailing up the Tiber, crossed the Apennines, and put out to sea to meet his final defeat in a place where he could direct it himself.

He had the ship drop anchor outside Ancona. There was no sign at all of either war or life for miles around, only the vultures circling over the deserted town.

The Pope waited.

On the 12th of August he established contact with twelve Italian ships which were seeking to join the last crusade.

Pius II called together the prelates, blessed them, and told them he would now hand over to them the task he had begun; they were to complete it, and a curse would fall on them if they shrank from God's work.

So he died, and was immediately transported back by water to Rome, his starting point.

In actual fact Pius II's starting point was a quite different one. It was known he was born in 1405 in Corsignano. What was not known, but what Lodovico's secretary, Marsilio Andreasi, found out was that Enea Silvio Piccolomini's mother was called Lucretia, and that his father was a soldier, a mercenary named Eurealus who disguised himself as a servant to gain admission to the small household of impoverished nobility in that Tuscan village. Or more precisely, he gained admission in the guise of a servant, for it was as a servant that Eurealus was employed; he was cook and gardener, without any salary other than Lucretia's favors. In addition, it appeared from the accounts that a good part of his soldier's salary had gone towards the expenses of the expanded ménage.

When the little Enea Silvio was born, he was placed out to nurse with a gardener near Siena, so that he should not disturb the peaceful relationship between Lucretia, Eurealus, and Menelaus.

It was not Lodovico but Barbara who had initiated this investigation. After all the disappointment occasioned to her by the Church — a disappointment she could hardly share with Lodovico as it would have left him quite simply delighted — she had taken Marsilio into her confidence and Marsilio, who had never become a priest himself, and had never dared show his poetry to anyone, had flung himself onto Piccolomini's corpse like a vulture from Ancona.

Once the corpse had been picked clean he agreed with Barbara that Nana should at all events be presented with the results. In order to be with her every day, Marsilio requested permission to help her when she fed Mantegna's peacocks. In the course of this task he won her confidence and contrived to make her see her father from a new angle. Eventually they were agreed that her father looked like a peacock trying in vain to secure to himself a proper share of "The Ghost Room" that he could call his own. He had thought he could be in control of his own destiny, while all the time he had without knowing it merely repeated his parents' history. Vanity of vanities! With some additions, of course. But they were also vanity! said Marsilio and listened mournfully to his own voice. That voice could have so easily belonged to a priest, if only he had not been so terribly disillusioned.

In the quiet of her own thoughts Nana went on to conclude that this repetition of history might have been part and parcel of her father's self-delusion.

Did he not put his son Piero in the care of a simple gardener just as he himself had been? And he would surely have been devastated when Piero, far from working his way up to a position of eminence in society, had actually contrived to sink even lower.

7

Nana now had five boys, whom she for the time being protected against the world while she taught them everything between heaven and earth.

From when they were very little they came to feed the peacocks. When they grew older and learned to write, Nana dictated:

"The peacock is a house bird. The peacock's tail feathers are the most beautiful feathers you can find. These feathers have magnificent blue and green colors with a metallic luster and the tip is supplied with a multicolored eye which cannot see anything. During the day they mostly live on the ground in the bushes; in the morning and evening they go out in the fields and open places to eat and drink what they can find. They spend the night sitting in trees. The peacock manages well when it has luck and once a day gets fresh green leaves."

The boys did not know their father. Nobody knew him. Only Nana. And she was not saying. But once a year, usually on one of the darkest nights of rain and wind, she would open the door to Piero who had crept in from the open fields where he otherwise lived his life.

The first time he came, she no longer recognized him. His hair was so overgrown he looked more like an animal than a person. In order to reveal his identity as the true Piero he had to ask her to find the orange in the chimney, the one in which he had secretly inserted her name with cloves. She found it and let him come in. The orange was pristine and Piero, who was terribly hungry, ate it immediately, name and all.

The person who writes another person's name on an orange and hangs it up in the darkness of the chimney is wishing death upon that other person.

There is nothing to indicate that Piero ever regretted this wish. Probably he had completely forgotten about it and only remembered because he needed to prove his love for Nana.

What he did not know, and what maybe none of them knew, was that the person who consumed such an orange put himself at risk of suffering the fate or meeting the death that has been wished upon the person whose name is inscribed on it.

Nana never told the boys about their father, but she told them many things about a person she had met once who sought to sink down to the lowest levels of society, who sought to live apart from other people and ventured his life on being admitted as a valid member of the animal kingdom, on a par with squirrels, hares, and foxes. And she told them about this person's life in a cave dug out of the mountains, where he had a parlor and a kitchen as well as a larder like every other animal on earth.

"So then we are also a kind of animal because we have a kitchen," said one of the boys. "Then he could just as well live in a house?"

"He's afraid of houses," said Nana.

"Why is that?"

"He's afraid that eventually houses will fill the whole earth, so there will no longer be room for fresh green leaves."

"He's not a peacock," said the boys.

"No, he is closer to being the opposite of a peacock," said Nana, "if that exists."

This was the kind of story they loved to hear, just as they loved to hear Lodovico tell about the war against the Turks. Particularly the story about the Turkish princess who was transformed into a butterfly. Lodovico had killed her husband and, according to Turkish custom, the victor was obliged to take care of the slain man's wife and children. Or more correctly, in the same moment that he killed the Turkish prince, the princess became his wife. This made Lodovico very unhappy because he already had a wife at home who was waiting for him. He did not know what he should do with the princess. There was no one who would buy her, no one who would have her as a free gift. Nobody would so much as touch her, but nevertheless they secretly made sure that she stayed close to Lodovico the whole time and came on board his ship when he was about to leave. It was not until they had raised anchor that Lodovico remembered a piece of advice he had received from one of the bundled-up old women on whom he had bestowed his silver knife and his sack of provisions.

"My master," she had said, "my master does not know the Turkish women, but if a man says to a Turkish woman that he will sacrifice his life for her, then she immediately transforms herself into a flea, a louse, or an ant, rather than wait in fear for the man to die."

Now Lodovico remembered this and he said to the Turkish princess: "I love you so much already that I will sacrifice my life for you!" In that very moment she was transformed, not into a flea, a louse, or an ant, but, wise as she was, into a butterfly which spread its wings and flew straight off towards Turkey. But the flight was apparently too long, for after some time the butterfly returned and clung to the foremast for the rest of the voyage. And when they reached Italy, the Turkish princess flew out to the flowering springtime land. Lodovico followed her with his eyes until she was a little tiny dot. Then he went home to his wife and ate dinner and told her everything that he had experienced in the war against the Turks.

"Also about the butterfly?" asked the boys, as they asked every time.

And every time Lodovico answered: "No, not about the butterfly. The butterfly is a secret. And you must promise me that you will never tell it to anyone."

The five boys promised, and the rest of the day they dashed around with their homemade nets trying to catch the Turkish princess.

When Piero was home he always devoted some of his time to giving Nana certain instructions for the boys' upbringing. He called his ideas democratic and said that they as parents had a duty to take pride in considering the boys all as one being. True enough, this one being moved in five separate parts, but since their movements were so completely coordinated, no importance at all could be attached to their being subdivided. His wish was that they should grow up as a symbol of humankind's inevitable unity, which he thought they best could further by emphasizing the outward likeness. Of course not everyone can be given the same appearance, but they can all be accorded the same rights and opportunities, the same chance of happiness.

Nana did not say anything. But she thought maybe this happiness was something children experienced only when they had a fever and snuggled up to each other, like nestlings that can tell a storm is on the way from the change in feather movements. So maybe Piero had the right ideas, and never mind where he got them from.

8

Nana often thought about Piero when she watched the boys play. Each time he had come home he had been more fanatical, but at the same time he had revealed his deep anxiety over the smallest thing, like a confused animal that notices winter is approaching but has forgotten what he is supposed to be doing about it.

Nana knew that when Piero grew old he would become shameless, cowardly, and irritable. She would not blame him, for she thought that without these characteristics, which most people agree to call bad, he would never have been as wonderful and surprising and genuinely childlike as he was. Nearly every day she feared for his life, and lately she had begun to pray to God that he would one day return to her forever, if not soon, then when he was tired or no longer had the power to find happiness and enjoyment in his life with the beasts of the fields.

But when Nana gave birth to her seventh son, she noticed a change in Piero which was not what she had expected.

First and foremost he was freshly washed, his hair was cut, and all those strips of hide he wore were lighter and more lustrous than when he had last visited her.

His appearance made her elated and expectant, and she immediately began to hope he had it in mind to stay at home. But every time she led the conversation in that direction, he fell silent as the grave, and the only result of her guarded hope was that he left several hours before sunrise, and she thought she had noticed in him an indifference, a covert hostility that she was afraid he could only escape if something ill befell him.

She did not know that such an accident had already occurred. One winter's day when he had been feeling sick during his daily wanderings, he lost his way owing to a sudden bout of fever and, instead of going north in the direction of his underground lair, he went south and in this way came too close to Mantua. He knew that he was approaching a town, but did not recognize it right away. When at last he did recognize it, he was already so weakened that he had to lie down to sleep on the bare earth in the shelter of a large rock.

When he woke, he lay there staring up at a sky-blue ceiling. At first he thought it was the sky, but then he realized he was lying in a large room with silk on the walls and fruit bowls and flowers on the tables closest to the bed. Next to him sat a woman; her head was half-veiled and she had smiling eyes. He clutched his head because he could not grasp anything at all, and he noticed that someone had washed him and cut his hair. He asked the woman where he was, but she indicated without a word but with flapping gestures that he was not to speak; he was to drink a little and eat some fruit if he could, or otherwise sleep and regain his strength so that everything would function as it should. When he saw that she meant him well, he fell asleep again for several days and nights, yes, even longer, until the sickness had left him.

The morning Piero woke up, quite recovered, the woman was gone. He sat up and looked around for his clothes, but they were nowhere to be found. Yet no sooner had he decided to get up and look for them than the woman returned, but this time she was not alone. By her side stood his father-in-law, Lodovico Gonzaga, looking like some kind of benevolent godfather.

"It was I who found you," he said, "that is, at first I did not know that it was you I had found, only that it was an exhausted person, attacked by an illness that would pull him down into the earth where he lay. It was not until Farfalla," he pointed to the woman, "had washed your face and combed out your hair that I saw it was you. It was a great shock, but a delightful one to find you alive."

"I'm very grateful," said Piero, "but I must say to you at once that it is impossible for me to return to Nana and live in her house. For many years we have had a very good arrangement with each other and the time when we can make a change in that is a long way off."

"I completely agree with you," said Lodovico. And he actually did. He was not interested in Nana's or the Gonzaga family's prestige being ruined by a husband returning home. Such was the miracle of the dwarf giving birth to angels that it could not take too many jolts before the hard facts of the matter must emerge.

Piero was surprised to discover in himself such a strong aversion to resuming his old life out with the beasts of the field. Was that all there was to it? Was it enough to be washed, trimmed, and pampered before you lost your way? Piero decided that he would bide his time and for the present accept Lodovico's offer to live with Farfalla on the understanding that he took care not to reveal his identity to anyone. Farfalla would see to his material needs while he in return would give her company during the many hours she had to be without Lodovico.

Every morning, at six o'clock, Lodovico paid a visit at the end of his regular walk in the countryside outside Mantua. After Piero had wondered for some time about this punctuality, Lodovico said one morning:

"I myself gave Farfalla her name—she is a butterfly."

And then he told Piero that she was the Turkish princess whom he had long ago been obliged to bring back with him to Italy; here he had secretly settled her into this pavilion in Buonaccolsi's garden. This is where she has lived ever since, absorbed in her memories, without seeing or talking to anyone save for Lodovico, until circumstances brought Piero into the picture.

After turning this information over in his mind for a couple of days Piero realized what it meant for himself: that his life from now on was tied to Farfalla's, that under no circumstances would Lodovico let him slip away, because he feared the secret about the Turkish princess would then be revealed and that would be the end of their covert existence. This existence had by now become Lodovico's true life. Everything else was only the Prince's monotonous movements in the hinterland of economic realities.

9

Piero made his last two visits to Nana in peril of his life, and with them he brought the number of boys up to nine.

How great this danger was in reality nobody knew. Only Nicolosia. And she was dead. One September evening in 1472 she strayed into Buonaccolsi's garden. The next morning she was found dead near the well in the central courtyard of Mantegna's house.

The only thing Lodovico was bothered about in connection with this was the persistent rumors that Marsilio had taken the blame. But if it was worth the trouble, such rumors could easily be brushed aside since it was common knowledge that Marsilio was one of those romantic antiheroes who are always ready to accept the blame for anything.

The worst of it was, of course, that Marsilio really had done it. That is to say, Marsilio had forestalled Lodovico and committed the act, just as Lodovico was the one to throw Nicolosia out through Buonaccolsi's garden gate. There Marsilio was keeping watch and, wrongly assuming Nicolosia to be old Buonaccolsi's lover, he killed her and under the cover of darkness dragged her back into Mantegna's courtyard. Lodovico did not dare to make himself known. A trial was out of the question. Later, Lodovico often toyed with the idea of murdering Marsilio, but this always remained only a thought. Such sudden death could easily bring things up to the surface that were best kept hidden.

Thus, life in Mantua continued peacefully, and Lodovico tried with all of his might to alleviate the conditions in which the two lived shut up in the pavilion. Yes, he even gave his consent to their arranging things together as man and wife, always on condition that this did not disturb the precisely regulated mechanism of their life together. So far, so good! Until at last something decisive happened.

One morning in the summer, around ten o'clock, when Nana stepped out in the courtyard she saw all the boys, all nine of them, crawling around on top of two old women who had lain down in the grass. Her first thought was that all these white flapping angel children on the two black-veiled women looked like an omen. Whether it was an evil omen or a good one she could not decide straightaway. But when she heard the boys call the old women Grandmother and saw them munching oranges and lumps of sugar that had been distributed among them, she decided the omen was good.

The two women revealed themselves to Nana as the Maria sisters, the two white-clad women who had brought Pius II's greeting to Piero and Nana's wedding, as he had asked them to in his last letter from Ancona.

Now together they relived that happy wedding day, and Nana told about her life, her fruitfulness, and her uncertain hopes of coming to understand how her own and the boys' lives were a reflection of Piccolomini's life.

Not until evening did the two grandmothers reveal the real reasons for their visit. First they brought greetings from Piero's sister, Lucia, who had settled into her role as a female Antipope; she was living in Clusium, in a labyrinth that she had discovered, in the company of three devoted women friends. To sum up her message in a few words, she would say that she preached that no two things are alike, because unity is a divine platitude. The two grandmothers themselves also lived in Clusium and were quite content to clean the maze of passageways and repair those parts that had fallen into neglect.

Finally they came to their real business: they brought greetings from Piero.

Nana turned pale. She did not expect that there was anyone either in Mantua or anywhere else who knew that Piero was alive.

All right, it was not entirely his greetings because they had not spoken with Piero himself. But by chance they had arrived in Mantua at Nana's house just as Piero was leaving after his last visit. They had a suspicion there was something wrong when they saw that he did not move about uninhibitedly, but crept furtively past the houses from one hiding place to the next. They had shadowed him and with luck were able to steal after him into Buonaccolsi's garden, where they had hidden in a woodshed not used during the summer.

From this hiding place they watched Piero and Farfalla living as if in paradise, with the blessing and under the supervision of Lodovico in person.

Once delivered of this message, the Maria sisters took a deep breath and said, of course it was up to Nana to decide what should be done. That something should be done they apparently had no doubt. Their son had to be rescued, but how this was to be effected was not something they even wanted to think about.

But Nana did. Already in the course of the night she had conceived a plan. At daybreak she procured a

114

carriage for the two old women and, once she had fed everyone a solid meal, she sent them on their way to Clusium with all the boys who basked in the fairy-tale light, like godchildren who for the first time feel humanity's attention resting upon them.

Then Nana cleaned her house, once again read "The Angels' Book," went over her plan for the next day, and lay down to sleep so early that she knew she would wake up at sunrise.

It was a morning of clear pale sky. The land was still black with, here and there, a first hint of color. Nana set out in silence for Buonaccolsi's garden where she placed herself behind the dense jasmine to the left of the gate and waited. Only once a dog ran by, but did not find her, just lifted its leg by the bush and disappeared. From the castle she could hear the peacocks' crying. They were probably roosting in their favorite place in the trees along the south wall.

Lodovico came at exactly six o'clock. He looked old and seemed distrait, and Nana did not have the least difficulty sneaking in and hiding before he got the gate locked. She now waited in the woodshed until Lodovico had left again.

Then she crept up to the house and waited for Farfalla to go out into the kitchen to prepare the meal they were to eat at noon. When Piero was alone in the parlor, sitting on a cushion, staring out in front of him like an animal that has been abandoned by the pack, she went right up to him, lifted his face a bit, kissed him on the mouth, and drove a dagger into his heart.

Then she went out into the kitchen and asked Farfalla if there was anything she could help her with.

The next morning when, as usual, Lodovico walked into the house, he found Piero dead and the Turkish princess gone.

It had to happen sooner or later and so it happened today, the 19th of October 1478.

Lodovico lay down on the bed and opened his artery. And while the blood slowly drained out, he thought about the landscape he had walked through that morning, how it had been reclining under the sky as if no one had ever woken it, not the sun, not the rain, only the futile dreams that held nature in eternal balance, because the dreams (being dreams) insisted that the shadows should blossom, never the plants themselves. And because the plants, for this extraordinary purpose, could expend the energy of innumerable human thoughts and feelings instead of the sun's, the wind's and the rain's.

From this useless landscape, where throughout the century time and place have been whirling by without ever settling, he, Lodovico Gonzaga III, stepped into Buonaccolsi's garden and immediately it was as if a wakeful eye had watched each one of his steps. The eye of Death.

And he understood, while he quietly melted away, that this garden was in its own way just as superfluous as the landscape beyond; it resembled a drawing of a brain in cross section; all the passages looked like mazes, but they were indeed passages, if anyone took the trouble to follow them; all the mirror effects showed up on closer inspection to be the things themselves, yes, even the two halves of the brain, which seemed so completely similar, betrayed quite overwhelming differences, to such a degree that they were a wonder to behold. Why were the roses reddest in the east, and the lilies whitest in the west? In the north the carp were the fattest. In the south the disintegrating stone dogs pale and small. Why . . . ?

10

I am now living in Clusium, which possibly looks like that garden Lodovico tried to visualize as he lay dying.

We have given up our old names and are all of us called Maria. But when I have sat at my table and written about all of these more or less strange people, who in the course of time have entrusted themselves to me, then I still have in my secret heart continued to call myself Farfalla. Because it was she whom they all visited, and to her they told their stories of life in the city, even though Lodovico believed she was a secret. Me, I have never been a secret. But I have little by little been entrusted with all the possible secrets, and in these pages you will be able to read a part of them.

The rest I will save for myself. There are of course no grounds for hiding some of them any longer. Nana's secret, for example: all of her children were born of Lucia, but Piero, their father, put them out to nurse with her. Nana is happy, or wise. She now has a small apartment in miniature, exactly as small and comfortable as she has always wished it to be.

Other secrets I have had to give up discovering. The peacocks' for example.

III

MY SUMMER HOLIDAY

by Bernardino, 10 years old

We did not go anywhere for our summer holiday because my father has been working all the time and it is still not finished.

He is painting pictures on all the walls in a large room up in the castle, and I have been helping him mix paints and all the other things that need to be done because you cannot just start painting on the stone that is there.

First, we have to mix chalk and sand into a thick plaster which we quickly slap onto the wall and smooth out so it is neat. On top we put a layer that is finer, and we keep it damp the whole time, not wet, so you can just make a mark with your finger. My father gets furious if it is too wet or if it dries too quickly because then the colors cannot go into the plaster, he says, and all of it is ruined.

One day the plaster hardened before he had finished drawing the outlines and we were told to break it all up and start from the beginning.

I like mixing the paints best, even if they do not look right when they are in the pots. Not until they are up on the wall and sucked into the fresh plaster are they as they should be. It looks beautiful when the sky dries. You could think it was the real sky and that the walls had disappeared so you could look right out.

I am also the one who gets the milk every morning for the paint. I milk the goats myself, and when we are busy a lot of milk is needed.

My father said if I took care of the milk I would be allowed to try actually painting on the wall and not just on something that will not be used.

So I painted all the legs and some of the curtains and columns, not the patterns of course, but the ground color and that is at least as important as everything else because if it does not lie completely smooth it is impossible for the others to work with light and shade and perspective to get it to look natural.

This summer my father has had nine helpers besides me. The only things no one is allowed to help him with are the faces, the sky, and the landscapes in the background.

When they are to be painted, all of us are thrown out, and we sit in the courtyard playing board games, and if it lasts so long that the others begin to get drunk or fall asleep then I run over to talk with Marsilio. Marsilio loves me almost more than my father, but still I like my father best because he does not show it so much.

When the face is finished we are called back in. It

is best that we do not criticize anything right away because it could easily happen that my father throws the work aside, sometimes for several days. We should rather be enthusiastic until he begins to criticize one or another thing himself, and then we are sent out again until it is corrected and everybody is content.

One day we were kept outside all afternoon and all evening and all the helpers went home. I sat alone on the rock and waited right until it got dark. Then I went over to Marsilio because he was watching Gentilia, my little sister. Since my mother died, Marsilio often watches us and that is very interesting.

That evening he read us a story about the garden of paradise. I think he had written it himself, but we had not got far into it when suddenly we heard my father shouting out in the courtyard that he was finished. "Is no one there?" he shouted. Yes, I was there, and I bolted with such a speed I knocked over the young cook who is always listening outside Marsilio's door, and Gentilia was right on my heels.

So only the two of us were allowed to go in and see. It was almost completely dark and Gentilia was afraid, but then my father lit the lamps which he had blown out so he could surprise us better. And that he did. It was a fantastic town he had painted. It was white and set on a mountain top and the sky had real clouds, and in the front there stood a large tree with a forked branch, perfect for sitting in.

My father had tears in his eyes. "I wish your mother could see this," he said.

It was quite solemn and I was just about to cry, but then Gentilia wanted to be lifted up to see better and then I knew that Father would start laughing because he loved to hear Gentilia tell about the pictures, and she was already chattering away while my father held her fingers away from all the things she told about because they were not yet completely dry.

"When I become completely small and go all the way in there, into the picture our father has painted, then I would be just as small as all of the people who travel on the road, and then I would go in through the gate and live in the fine round house right in the middle and look out of all the windows to see if anyone is coming. And then I could make dinner for them. In the evening all the stonemasons would come up from the Land of the Dead and eat, but during the day they would cry so you could hear them all the way up in the air. If I dare, because of the captain, I will go down the road and shout to them that they should just come up even though it is not yet evening, because it is much better that they help me in the house and do kitchen work and mend my toys."

And so she continued like this the whole time, also while we walked home, and until she was in bed, yes, right until she fell asleep. "She is such a clever girl," my father said. "She knows everything, long before she has been told." "Maybe it's something she dreams," I said. "Dreams are necessary in any case," said my father. "If we don't have as many dreams at night as we have forkfuls of rice in the day, or bread, or all other possible things from honey to garlic, then we die. If we skip over a single dream or two, we become sickly and can no longer find our way around in the world with any sense of safety and joy."

What my father said had a big impact on me, but still I forgot all about it until I remembered I was supposed to write about my summer holiday, about a trip I have been on or an outing. That was this morning, the last day of holiday. And we still did not have time to go anywhere. Now it is the afternoon, so it will be too late if I first take a trip and then write about it. Therefore, I have decided first to write about a trip while I pretend in my mind that I have left on it, as in a dream. Then the future will decide if one day I make the same journey in reality. Or maybe only one like it.

The journey I will now begin is Gentilia's, into my father's picture. I do not think there are very many people in Mantua who have ever been in a town as strange as the incredible town I visited today, the 27th of August 1473.

I set out right away. It is peaceful and green on all sides and I climb up towards the high town with great expectation. But I am not very high up before I realize something or other is different, something that cannot be made out because I have never seen it before. Now I come to the forked tree and climb up and sit in it: I have to find out what is wrong. But I cannot see anything. The trees are all the usual trees I know so well; the houses are houses like those in Mantua or like those the architects draw or like the ones we found in the spring when the school was out on a dig; the fields are green, the sky is blue, and the rocks have the usual brownish, bluish, or greenish colors; even the tiny people, whom I hope to meet, look completely natural. Yet I cannot get away from the thought that something is wrong. The atmosphere is wrong as when you kill a chicken and it runs around without its head.

I climb down and move on. When I am up the road over the largest quarry, I stop. At this point I have already passed quite a few smaller quarries and underground shafts, but it is not until I reach this place close to the rocks and have a view of the whole area where the stonemasons have worked their way into the wonderful marble, that I realize what it is that is different:

The mountain has been made by people. Not only

the town up on the very top, with its walls and forts and everything that is normally built by people, but the whole enormous mountain that lifts the town up into the light, it is all made by people, made from the ground up, foot by foot, so the stones look almost real, they almost have the same odd shapes, almost the same sheen as real stone, or natural stone.

It is beyond me. Have these stonemasons' forefathers taken thousands of years to build up this mountain, only for their descendants to open it up and mine the stone again?

And where have they got the stone from? Have they fetched it from another place? Or have they also made the stone themselves? If the stone we usually call stone is the real stone, then this stone is not real and natural or divine. The stone I am now touching is a human stone. At one time there were people, here on this spot, who not only produced the mountain, but also produced the stone that the mountain is made of.

I walk up to the red gate tower to ask to go in past the sloping wall between the captain's fortress and the city wall itself. To the left of the tower a ruin has been built with short columns and low arches of rough-hewn stones. I do not think the rest of this building has ever existed. I am sure it was built as a ruin by people who knew that ruins should remind them of something, but did not know what they should remind them of. To the right there is a steep slope planted with trees, with five or six large blocks of marble, columns, pyramids, and vats, all made of the same man-made marble as the one I am walking on. It occurs to me that these people must have known what is needed to create history, but they have forgotten the history itself or never had any idea about its existence.

The soldiers' washing is hanging on both sides of the tower to dry in the sun, but otherwise there is no sign of life. The people I saw from my viewing place in the tree have all disappeared, and it is completely quiet when I step into the gatehouse, not even a guard, not even a dog comes out, although I stand and scrape my feet against the worn stones.

Then I hear something rustling in the garden. It sounds like a wild boar digging in the dirt. I go closer and the boar comes and sniffs me as if it were the watchdog. Then it goes and lies down with the hind and the bull that are sleeping over in the corner where the grass between the paving stones is highest. There is also an ox standing and munching, and a couple of horses drinking water from a tub next to the well. All of these animals must have lived here in the court-yard for years, for everywhere there are mountains of manure heaped up, and there is a frightful stink. Just as I begin to think of hurrying towards the white palace I notice an old man sitting over near the wall; he is making signs to me.

He looks very weak and all he is wearing is an old lion skin with the fur nearly all worn off. On a little rug next to him lie a very lifelike snake head, a tarnished belt, and some apples made out of some sort of metal. I right away think he will try to get me to buy these treasures, but he only points to his mouth and to the well, and so of course I get him some water.

When he has drunk it, I ask him where I can find the captain.

"That is me," he whispers and bids me to sit down on the ground at his feet.

"I would like to have admittance," I say, "to the green glacis."

"Yes, I would be delighted to give you admittance," says the old man, "but I have my orders."

"What orders?"

"It has been ages since I got them," he says, and he looks resigned.

"From whom?" I ask.

"I cannot remember," he says as if that were the answer he always gives for everything.

I do not get anywhere with him but continue anyway: "Is there nothing I can do to get into the town?"

"You can do nothing. Only I can do anything."

"And what can you do; maybe I can help you?"

"I cannot do anything," he says crossly. "I have orders never to let any strangers in before I have gone away with all my things and all my animals and taken them back to the places where I have brought them from."

"Is that all?" I ask with enthusiasm. "I would like to help you. Where do they go?"

"I do not know where they go. I cannot remember where they go. Neither the hind, the wild boar, nor the ox. I do not know where I caught them. It is hundreds upon hundreds of years ago. The only thing I can do is sit here and be immortal with these dumb creatures. It is all a terrible mess."

"Yes, it is a horrid smell," I say just to say something friendly while I stand there thinking about something else. "What is your name?"

"I cannot remember. And I have also got used to the stench. And so has the dog."

"You have a dog?"

"Yes, it is lying over there, sleeping in the manure."

"What is its name?"

"I cannot remember. But it does not matter because it never leaves me. It simply cannot be bothered. It cannot even bring itself to bark. It was a dreadful sight, you know, when it used to bark, because it has three heads and when all three heads barked at once, all hell was let loose."

"Cerberus," I whisper. I have heard about it so often. Both my father and Marsilio have told about how it guards the innermost gate to the underworld. "Cerberus!" I yell. And now the old dog comes to us and licks us both at one time with its three red tongues.

"You know its name," said the old man, pleased. "Cerberus," he says scratching it behind the many ears.

"Yes, and I also know what your name is," I say.

"What, then?"

"Your name is Hercules."

"Yes, I am sure it is, when you say it. I cannot remember anything myself. The only thing I remember is we crossed over the river of forgetfulness and then we had to work out everything else for ourselves, it was said, and here I have sat ever since. Do you say that the dog has to be taken to the underworld?"

"Yes, and the golden apples have to be returned to the Hesperides, the belt is Hippolyta's and the manure has to be taken to King Augeas's stables which you once cleared it away from."

Old Hercules already looks hundreds of years younger with the thought that finally something is happening, no matter what, and we help each other load the manure onto the old soldiers' carts. Hercules sweeps it up with Hippolyta's belt, and the work goes like child's play. When the courtyard is completely clean, the bull and ox and horses are hitched to the carts. The hind and wild boar go together in front with Hercules and the dog. Hercules has tucked the belt, golden apples, and snake head under his old lion skin. When the procession is ready a huge flock of birds flies down from the trees and perches on top of the carts. Now I remember them. They are the huge cannibal birds from Stymphalus that flap their wings and yearn for how they used to be, before they were defeated.

"You just begin to go down into the underworld," I say, "then all the rest will fall into place."

"That is easy enough," he says, full of trust in the future. "I have a friend who went down there last week. The entrance lies just down there in the first quarry."

"What is your friend's name?" I ask, hoping his memory is returning.

"I cannot remember," he says. "But he went down there last week. A little girl came by and gave him a flute and then off he went."

"And where did the girl go?" I asked.

"She went into the town. With very small children it has always been different. They are allowed in anywhere. They know everything beforehand and they understand how to speak in riddles, so they reveal nothing. This girl said nothing. She just handed over the flute to my friend and no sooner had she gone into the town than the soldiers and stonemasons left their work and followed her. As far as I understand, she settled into the fine round house that sits in the middle."

Hercules points out the house for me and we bid each other a heartfelt farewell. Then I go up the last stretch towards the town while realizing I forgot to tell him he is a hero. But maybe that is not the thing to tell him now when all his heroic deeds must be undone again. That is very likely the most difficult task that can be given to the immortals.

I go into the town, no one stops me, and make my way to the round house. It buzzes with life and when I step in I see that, in reality, it is a large theater. Right down in the middle of the stage is my sister, Gentilia, making a meal for all the soldiers and stonemasons and all the other people, including the women and children who have been streaming in.

"Come in and join the party," an old woman says to me.

"What is the party for?" I ask.

"We are waiting for her mother and father," the woman says, pointing to Gentilia.

I try to make my way to Gentilia to learn what she is up to, but just as I am about to reach her, the talking stops, the eating stops, and through the stillness a flute can be heard, while everyone holds their breath and gets weepy-eyed, so given over are they to their thoughts and feelings. The flute comes closer and closer and soon it drifts in through the entrance of the house, and after it a man comes, and behind him, a woman. The man is playing the flute.

As soon as they enter the house the rejoicing breaks loose. Orpheus, Orpheus! We see Orpheus sink into his lover's arms and everyone rushes to carry the reunited couple down to the center of the party.

Then I feel Gentilia tap me on the arm.

"It is Father," she says. "He has brought our mother home again."

"Yes," I say. "I knew it could be done. When Hercules and all the other heroes begin their return, then we can begin the new stories."

"I love stories," says Gentilia. "Come, let us go to our mother and get her to tell us all about how our father was able to bring her back to the world."

Which world? I think. But I do not say it.